CLUELESS

A Pier 70 Novella
NICOLE EDWARDS

By Nicole Edwards

Alluring Indulgence Series

Kaleb
Zane
Travis
Holidays with the Walker Brothers
Ethan
Braydon
Sawyer
Brendon

The Walkers of Coyote Ridge Series

Curtis
Jared
Hard to Hold
Hard to Handle
Beau

Austin Arrows Series

Rush
Kaufman

Club Destiny Series

Conviction
Temptation
Addicted
Seduction
Infatuation
Captivated
Devotion
Perception
Entrusted
Adored
Distraction

Dead Heat Ranch Series

Boots Optional
Betting on Grace
Overnight Love
Jared

By Nicole Edwards (cont.)

Devil's Bend Series

Chasing Dreams
Vanishing Dreams

Office Intrigue Series

Office Intrigue
Intrigued Out of the Office
Their Rebellious Submissive
Their Famous Dominant
Their Ruthless Sadist

Pier 70 Series

Reckless
Fearless
Speechless
Harmless
Clueless

Sniper 1 Security Series

Wait for Morning
Never Say Never
Tomorrow's Too Late

Southern Boy Mafia/Devil's Playground Series

Beautifully Brutal
Without Regret
Beautifully Loyal
Without Restraint

Standalone Novels

Unhinged Trilogy
A Million Tiny Pieces
Inked on Paper
Bad Reputation
Bad Business

Naughty Holiday Editions

2015
2016

Clueless

Pier 70, 5

NICOLE EDWARDS

Nicole Edwards Limited
PO Box 806
Hutto, Texas 78634
NicoleEdwardsLimited.com

CLUELESS – A Pier 70 novella is a work of fiction. Names, characters, businesses, places, events and incidents either are the products of the author's imagination or used in a fictitious manner. Any resemblance to actual persons, living or dead, business establishments, events, or locals is entirely coincidental.

Cover Image: © Wander Aguiar | wanderbookclub.com
Cover Models: Kaz Vander & Rachel B.

Cover Design: © Nicole Edwards Limited
Editing: Blue Otter Editing | BlueOtterEditing.com

ISBN (ebook): 978-1-939786-96-8
ISBN (print): 978-1-939786-95-1

Contemporary Romance
Mature Audiences

One

HOW MILLY MET GANNON

Eleven years ago

MILLICENT "IF YOU call me Millicent, I'll break your nose" Holcomb wasn't sure what she was thinking when she answered the ad for an administrative assistant position. Perhaps it was a moment of insanity.

Or sheer desperation.

Yeah. Probably the latter.

She'd applied at every retail business she'd come across with no luck, so she had moved on to administrative work. And she found an up-and-coming gaming company of all things.

For heaven's sake, she wanted a career in fashion, and based on the looks of the kids—because they couldn't be more than eighteen if they were a day—sprawled out in the tiny box of an office, she knew she was as far from a Paris runway as she could possibly get.

Seriously. The sheer volume of khaki pants should've been outlawed. Not to mention all the T-shirts with Star Trek references.

Then again, if she didn't want to move back in with her dad, which she absolutely did not, and she wanted to eat, which she definitely did, Milly knew she had to do something. This was her last chance before she broke down and applied at a fast-food restaurant. It wasn't that she was above working a cash register or cooking food, but she wasn't sure which was worse, hanging out with this group of tech nerds or wearing a hair net and asking if you wanted fries with that.

"Millicent?"

Milly cringed, digging her nails into her palm as she forced a smile and looked up. The king of gaming nerds was standing there, staring at her. The guy was handsome, she'd give him that. In a hot-nerd sort of way. It was the glasses, she decided. Those added that studious appeal.

He took a second to push the black-rimmed spectacles up on his nose before lifting one dark eyebrow.

Right. He was waiting for her to respond.

"Milly," she answered, getting to her feet.

Why had she worn the four-inch pumps again?

The man held out his hand and Milly returned the gesture, slipping her fingers into his firm grip.

Instantly she knew the extra effort she'd put into getting dressed for this interview was for naught. Her gaydar was shrieking loudly in her head.

Nope. She hadn't needed any additional lip gloss and mascara this morning, because this guy did not care one way or the other that she'd had her roots touched up or that red was a good color for her.

Then again, Milly was as professional as the next twenty-two-year-old wannabe fashion designer. If nothing else, her appearance would help to put him at ease and possibly make him believe she was cut out for ... whatever he would need her to do.

"Gannon Burgess," he said by way of introduction.

"Nice to meet you."

He nodded slightly, then motioned toward a small cubicle on the far side of the room. "Don't mind the mess. We just moved in here a few weeks ago. Still getting it all set up."

Milly peered around.

She would admit that she knew absolutely nothing about the gaming industry. According to the expensive equipment scattered about, gracing the surface of every secondhand desk and duct-tape-doctored chair, it was clear where the money was spent.

"It's a nice place," she lied easily, forcing another smile.

Gannon pushed his glasses up on his nose as he turned to face her. "Yeah? I was thinking it was a step above a cardboard box in the back alley, but what do I know?"

That earned a choked laugh from her, and for the first time since she'd woken up that morning, Milly felt some of the tension in her shoulders ease. "Okay, yes. You'd probably find more high-end furnishings by staking out the Walmart back alley, in fact."

Oops. Had she really said that out loud?

"I'll keep that in mind," he chuckled, turning back toward the cubicle. "Maybe that can be your first duty."

"Don't underestimate my dumpster-diving abilities, Mr.—" She racked her brain to remember what he'd said his last name was. Ah, crap.

"Call me Gannon, please."

"Gannon," she muttered, assigning the name to memory.

"As a rule, I underestimate no one. It's the safest way not to find yourself booted out on your ass," he said beneath his breath.

Milly figured there was a story there, but since she really wanted this job, she quelled her curiosity for the time being. If she was lucky and this geeky gamer decided to hire her, she'd have plenty of time to play Twenty Questions.

"So, can you tell me about your experience?" he prompted, taking a seat in the worn leather chair that sat behind a scarred metal desk. It was like the ones that every teacher in her high school had sat behind.

Milly lowered herself into the hard side chair, praying that the stain on the back did not rub off on her white jacket.

"It says here that you have administrative experience."

Milly crossed her legs and rested her hands on her knees, grinning. "If you call answering phones at a nail salon an administrative position, then yes, I've got all the experience you could possibly want."

The man studied her.

Although she'd been nervous when she woke up this morning, this guy quickly put her at ease. For one, he wasn't staring at her chest like he wanted to go diving in her cleavage and spend a week swimming in the depths. And two, he seemed to be as nervous about this interview as she was.

"If you don't mind me asking, what exactly is it you're looking for?" she asked, trying to relax her shoulders yet still look somewhat professional.

His left eyebrow did a little lift/tilt thing that she found endearing. "I honestly wish I knew."

Milly couldn't help but smile. "Would it require me to answer phones?"

"Yes."

"I'm good with phones." Adding a slightly breathless quality to her tone, Milly said, "Thanks for calling…" She peered around briefly, looking for anything that would tell her the name of the company. Quickly waving it off, she continued, "How may I direct your call?" She smiled. "Oh, you'd like to talk to Gannon? Yeah. Well, he's busy playing games right now, but I'm sure when he's finished, he'll be happy to return your call so you can chat about … game stuff."

Gannon leaned back in his chair, grinning from ear to ear. "You're hired."

Milly's eyebrows shot up into her hairline. "What if I have more questions for you?"

Gannon's smile dropped like a rock. "Do you?"

She shook her head. "No." Milly turned up the dial on her grin. "I'll take it."

With a laugh, Gannon leaned forward, resting his forearms on the desk. "Good. When can you start?"

"Yesterday."

"Perfect. Because I've got plenty of stuff from yesterday that I haven't gotten to yet."

"Really?"

He looked contrite. "You have no idea what you got yourself into."

Milly laughed. "I could say the exact same to you, Gannon."

Two

HOW MILLY AND AJ MET

May 29, 2016

AJ BALLARD STEPPED into the banquet room, his eyes searching the masses to find someone he recognized. There weren't many, but he hadn't expected there to be. He was his brother Hudson's plus one at this shindig, which meant he was the odd man out.

It only took a minute to locate Hudson, who was standing by the wall, his eyes locked on someone across the way. With a grin, AJ headed for the bar and asked for two glasses of water. When the bartender passed them over, he offered his thanks, then marched over to the big, brooding man in the corner.

"Hey, bro. What's up?"

Hudson's eyes cut over to him briefly.

They'd boarded the ship roughly an hour before and rather than race down to join the festivities, AJ had opted for a shower. He fully expected this trip to be full of activities because Hudson had already told him Gannon's best friend/assistant was in charge and she wasn't one to have everyone sitting around on their thumbs. Being that he was hoping to get a little downtime out of this cruise, AJ figured he'd take it where he could.

And now here he was, in a room filled with strangers, all of them there to celebrate the upcoming nuptials of Cam Strickland and Gannon Burgess, who would be wed in just a few short days.

AJ held up the two glasses of water—he wasn't much for drinking, and neither was his brother—allowing Hudson to take one.

"You good?" AJ cast a curious glance at his brother, wondering why the frown.

As usual, Hudson answered with a simple nod before sipping his drink. The man might've thought he could pull one over on AJ, but he knew better. His little brother—if thirty-five years old could be considered little—couldn't hide shit from him. Especially not when it came to his interest in one particular blond Hudson worked with.

"So, where's this boy toy of yours?" he asked just to get a rise out of Hudson.

It worked. His brother flipped him off. He hadn't expected anything less. Considering his brother was mute and couldn't speak, his hands did all his talking for him.

When it was obvious he wasn't going to get anything more from Hudson, AJ grinned. "Okay, fine. My turn." AJ's gaze strayed across the room until he located the sexy blonde he'd noticed talking to Cam, the owner of the marina Hudson worked at, a few minutes ago. "Who's the blonde? She single?"

Hudson's head snapped toward him, his eyes widening as he quickly jerked his head from side to side. AJ got the distinct feeling he wasn't answering, per se.

"What does that mean? She's not single?"

After setting his glass on a nearby table, Hudson started signing a response. You do not want to mess with Milly.

"Milly, huh?" He peered over at her again, admiring the pretty blonde in the sexy red sundress that showcased her tanned legs and her toned arms. Her hair was piled up on her head in some fancy knot, and her eyes crinkled when she laughed. She was, by far, the most beautiful woman in the room. "Interesting name."

He wondered what it was short for. Unless it was simply an off-the-wall nickname, there were only a few possibilities. Of course, he could only think of one, but the woman did not look like a Mildred. Not at all.

AJ turned back to his brother when Hudson punched him in the arm.

No, not interesting. Nothing about her is interesting. Leave her alone.

AJ laughed. "Since it seems to me that you're trying to warn me away from her, I'm gonna assume she's single."

Not warning you away from her. Her away from you.

"Oh, come on." It'd been a long damn time since a woman had caught his attention the way Milly had. For whatever reason, he couldn't take his eyes off her. Every move she made seemed oddly erotic in nature, calling to him on a completely cellular level.

Now he had to figure out how to introduce himself without coming on too strong. If he was lucky, and she wasn't too busy, perhaps they could spend some quality time together while they were stranded on this ship for the next seven days.

Hudson elbowed him, then signed: Seriously.

"I promise, I'll be good," AJ assured him. "Plus, it looks to me like you've got someone who could keep you pretty busy if you'd stop pretending you didn't want to bang his brains out."

AJ walked away on that note, not waiting to get a retort from Hudson. He knew his brother was fighting every urge inside him when it came to the man who worked alongside him at Pier 70. AJ had known for a while that Hudson was interested in Teague Carter, but for some reason, he was fighting it.

While Hudson might have all the time in the world to hold out, AJ didn't. At the ripe young age of thirty-seven, AJ wasn't getting any younger.

Figuring now was as good a time as any to congratulate the couple gearing up for their nuptials, AJ headed toward them.

Cam noticed him first, a smile on his face as AJ approached.

"Glad you could make it, AJ," he greeted. "You've met Gannon."

AJ shook Gannon's hand. "Good to see you again."

"Likewise," Gannon stated. His face had a slight green tinge to it, and AJ had to wonder if he was experiencing motion sickness.

Cam continued, "And this is Gannon's assistant, Milly Holcomb."

"That's all I am?" she said with a huff. "Here I was thinking I was his best friend, the one who keeps him in line, who ensures he goes where he needs to go when he needs to go there. And most importantly, the woman ultimately responsible for the two of you getting together." Her eyes widened. "Shall I go on?"

Cam chuckled. "Not necessary." He peered back at AJ. "AJ, this is Milly."

Unable to resist, AJ turned his full attention on the beautiful, sassy blonde. "It's a pleasure to meet you, Milly."

Her smile was radiant, transforming her from beautiful to downright gorgeous. Those ruby-red lips beckoned him to step closer, but he fought the urge. He'd just met her, after all.

"Likewise," she said sweetly, a gleam in her bright blue eyes. "I hear you're Hudson's plus one?"

"That I am," he admitted. "What kind of brother would I be if I refused to accompany him on a cruise to the Bahamas?"

"There are certainly worse things," she teased.

True. When Hudson had originally asked, AJ thought for sure the man was kidding. But, come to find out, Hudson had been serious about bringing him along, so here he was.

"Is it your first time on a ship?" she asked.

Cam caught AJ's eye, nodding his head as he took Gannon's hand and slipped away while Milly was otherwise preoccupied.

"No," AJ said seamlessly. "And hopefully not my last, either. I tend to go at least once every couple of years."

"A man of the world?"

"You could say that," AJ admitted with a smirk, enjoying the way Milly's eyes casually raked over him.

"So you haven't settled down yet?"

AJ grinned at her obvious fishing expedition. He hoped like hell that meant she was interested. "Nope. You?"

Milly waved a perfectly manicured hand, the color on her nails matching her dress and her lips. "Not a chance. I'm the kinda girl who ends up with the bad boy, and while it's fun to entertain them, they're always looking for the next best thing."

AJ was suddenly grateful for the idiots in her past. Anyone who would pass her up had to be out of their mind.

And fine, AJ knew more about Milly than he would let on. Being that she was Gannon's best friend, he'd heard plenty of stories about her in the past year. Since Cam and Gannon had hooked up, they'd spent quite a bit of time at the marina. Because his brother worked there, AJ spent as much time with Hudson as he could, and quite a few of those hours were on the lake. When AJ wasn't out of town on business, that was. And during that time, he'd heard plenty about the feisty blonde.

Milly's eyes shifted away from him. She'd just realized Cam and Gannon had slipped away. AJ made a mental note to thank them later.

"So, what does AJ stand for?"

"Aaron James," he said simply. "And Milly? It's short for…?"

"I'd tell you, but then I'd have to kill you," she said, flashing her pearly white teeth.

He laughed. The girl had spunk. He liked that. "Have it your way," he said with a grin. "But don't blame me if I end up calling you something else during the heat of the moment." He purposely looked away. "A decent turnout, yeah?"

Milly cleared her throat and it was followed by a soft laugh. He glanced her way and noticed her smiling. At least she hadn't shot him down yet.

"So far, so good." Her bright blue eyes locked on his face. "Looks as though all the important people have arrived."

Was he included in that count? Did she consider him to be important? For something other than the wedding, maybe?

"Well, as much as I'd love to stay and chat," she said with a one-thousand-megawatt smile, "I really do need to keep the grooms-to-be from wandering too far."

AJ hated to let her leave, but he understood. "Well, I hope to see you again. Maybe I could buy you a drink. You know, when you're not keeping everyone in line."

"Maybe," she said with a coy grin. "Better chance of that passionate moment that way."

Her witty comeback made him laugh out loud. "Noted."

She continued to smile. "It was great to finally meet you, AJ."

AJ nodded, then watched as she turned to leave. When Milly glanced back over her shoulder, he ensured they made eye contact again. Although he'd expected this to be an interesting adventure, he damn sure hadn't expected this little twist.

And he hoped like hell he'd have the opportunity to get to know Milly more during the trip. A whole lot more.

*

The next night

BAD BOYS, BAD boys, whatcha gonna do?

For whatever reason, that snippet was in her head, and Milly couldn't shake it. Ever since AJ had come out to join them at the pool, she'd been overwhelmed by inappropriate thoughts. Some were questions. Like, what did he look like naked? Was he good with his tongue? Did he have hidden jewelry on certain parts of his body?

Yep, she was a lost cause. It happened whenever she was attracted to someone. More so when that someone looked like AJ. The guy was sin on a stick, she could tell simply by the way he walked. Tall, lean, and packed with muscle, he was the sort you noticed when he walked into a room.

Didn't help that she was tipsy. Probably from the margaritas, but it could've been from how close she was to AJ. The man smelled good. Leather and musk, a scent ripe with pheromones that had her body singing.

From the second that man stepped into the banquet room yesterday afternoon, Milly had been hyperaware of him. It was as though she was drawn to him by one of those weird sci-fi forces Gannon was always including in his video games.

Of course, that wasn't at all surprising. AJ Ballard was a bad boy, and everyone knew Milly was attracted to that particular brand of man. The tattoos that marked his bulging biceps and his thick chest, the way he carried himself as though he was aware every woman on this big boat wanted a piece of him … AJ had it going on. And maybe not every woman on this ship wanted what he was packing, but Milly had noticed several looking his way. Oddly enough, it made her feel territorial. As though she should perch in his lap to keep them from eye-fucking him from afar.

Nice thought, but not a good idea.

The issue was, Milly knew what AJ would be good for. A few naked hours, some earth-shattering sex, a handful of wicked orgasms, and then a promise to call her later. It was always the same with his type. And she'd gotten adept at spotting them. In fact, she wondered if she had some sort of radar that homed in on them when they were within a certain distance.

"What's on your mind, beautiful?"

AJ's deep baritone caressed her skin, leaving goose bumps in its wake. Even the way he called her beautiful didn't sound cheesy the way it did when some men said it. She glanced over to see AJ watching her from his spot on the lounge chair beside hers. They were close enough Milly would've been able to reach out and run her fingernail over the dips and valleys of his abdomen.

Not that she would, but it was a damn nice fantasy.

He held out a fresh margarita before taking her empty glass and moving it to another table.

"Are you trying to get me drunk, Mr. Ballard?"

AJ chuckled. "Only if it it's a prelude to that passionate moment we were talking about yesterday."

There was no way to miss that he was flirting with her. Then again, she was laying on the charm just as thickly. But it was nice in a way. He was straightforward, not dancing around what this was.

"It's still early," she said, hoping he didn't see how flush he made her simply by breathing. "We'll have to see how the rest of the evening goes."

"Yeah? It is a nice night, huh?"

Better now that he was there. Not that she would tell him as much. However, if he continued to ply her with tequila, it was possible she would end up blurting it out. On a good day, the filter between her brain and her mouth was spotty at best. When she'd been drinking, it all but disintegrated.

"So, tell me about you," Milly probed, sipping her drink as slowly as she could to keep from jumping him.

"What do you wanna know?" His head turned as he stared over at her, those intense green eyes focused solely on her.

Everything. Milly wanted to know everything about this man.

That was her curse, though. Whenever she met someone new, a million questions bombarded her brain. She had an inquisitive nature.

"Let's start with how old you are." Simple, easy. Hopefully like him.

AJ smirked. "I'll answer your questions, but you've got to answer them, too."

"Fair enough," she agreed.

"Thirty-seven."

"I'll be thirty-three in a couple of days." Milly took another sip. "What is it that you do?"

"I work for a tech company. Software and storage," he said as though it was nothing. "I manage some of the corporate accounts. A lot of them in California. I spend quite a bit of time out there."

Ah, so he really was a man of the world. Milly wasn't sure how she felt about that. Then again, it meant she could probably let her guard down and spend a couple nights with him. What would it hurt? They could have some fun, and when they hit dry land at the end of the cruise, they could go their separate ways. No harm, no foul.

Sounded good.

In theory.

Two hours later, Milly had completely abandoned her getting-to-know-AJ quest in favor of seducing him. It seemed with every sensual word that came out of his mouth, Milly inched closer and closer to throwing her clothes off and impaling herself on him.

Hussy.

Granted, she was drunk from the margaritas and she'd noticed he hadn't had a single drink. She knew Hudson didn't drink, either, so she had assumed there was probably a little history there. Not that she questioned it. She didn't need to know the skeletons in his closet just to get in his shorts.

In fact, she wanted to get him out of his shorts. Soon.

They had spent the past two hours laughing, talking, getting the social niceties out of the way. They'd shared enough information to make a one-night stand not entirely awkward. And now that they'd made it back to her cabin, Milly found it nearly impossible not to touch him. Especially when he had her backed up against the wall, his forest-green eyes perusing her face as though he was studying her.

"I should go," he whispered.

Not wanting him to follow through on that threat, Milly threw her arms around his neck. "You should stay."

His eyes searched hers as though he thought she might change her mind with her next breath. Milly didn't play hard to get. It never worked out in her favor. Plus, she was the type of girl who went after what she wanted. There was no rule book that said only men could have fun when it came to brief sexual encounters. And she wasn't about to apologize for it.

"I was hoping you'd say that." His head lowered, his lips hovering just out of reach. His hand curved over her cheek. "What am I gonna do with you, Milly?"

That was easy. "Whatever you want."

When his lips finally met hers, Milly sighed, her entire body igniting. The heat of his chest, the delicious friction of his tongue, the heady scent of his skin … they overwhelmed her. She was drawn to him in a way she'd never been to any other man. What it was about Aaron James Ballard, she didn't know, but she was anxious to find out.

Milly could feel his hesitation, knew he was trying not to rush things. It was possibly a first for her. Most men were eager to get her out of her clothes, not caring how they got there or whether she was enjoying herself.

AJ was different. He was attentive. As though her pleasure mattered more than his own.

It took a few minutes, but Milly finally managed to urge him backward until they tumbled onto her bed. Their lips remained fused as their hands roamed, seeking, searching. She liked the hard, warm weight of him as he hovered over her, his thigh pressed intimately between hers.

Without waiting for an invitation, Milly managed to untie her bikini top before tossing it onto the floor. Since he was topless, it seemed only fair.

AJ lifted his head, his gaze zeroing in on her bare breasts. The look in his eyes was fierce, his need apparent. It amped up her desire, making her feel powerful.

His eyes darted up to her face briefly before his head lowered and his raspy tongue caressed one nipple, causing it to draw up tight.

"Fuck, you're responsive," he whispered. "And so fucking sexy."

When he wrapped those beautiful lips around her nipple, Milly moaned softly, encouraging him to continue. Her hands roamed over his back, smooth, warm skin teasing her palms. Unable to resist, Milly pivoted her hips, the friction of his thigh against her pussy bringing her entire body to life.

"AJ … oh, yes." God, his mouth was sheer perfection. The way he teased her nipples, alternating so that one didn't get more attention than the other… It was utter perfection.

He lifted his head, staring down at her, his eyes flashing with heat. "Christ, woman."

AJ placed his fingertip between her breasts, then trailed it lower until he hooked her bikini bottoms. He was watching her while she watched him. The moment was intense, far more than she expected. As though something deeper was passing between them.

She shook it off. Wishful thinking. This was a one-night encounter. Maybe two. No more than three. After that, Milly would put him out of her mind just the way he would do with her.

When he tugged her bottoms, lifting them from her skin, Milly inhaled sharply.

"I wanna taste you," he said softly. "I wanna feel your pussy on my tongue."

Oh, man. This guy was going to have her coming out of her skin if he kept that up. She'd always been a sucker for dirty talk. Milly enjoyed the verbal assault almost as much as the physical.

"What're you waiting for?" she teased, sliding her hands up to his face.

A second later, his lips lowered to her chest and he was kissing his way down her body. His thigh disappeared, leaving her feeling eager and empty. Thankfully, AJ wasn't one to leave her wanting. Within seconds, he rid her of the rest of her bathing suit and his warm mouth descended on her needy flesh. His tongue scraped over her clit, making her back bow.

Yes to the tongue question from earlier. The man certainly knew how to use his wicked tongue. He worked her easily. No rushing, either. AJ took his time, driving her to the brink over and over, making lights flash behind her eyelids as she succumbed to the overwhelming pleasure.

"You wanna come for me, beautiful?" he asked, his voice rough, caressing her skin as easily as his tongue did.

"Not yet," she told him. "Not until I have my turn."

AJ crawled back over her, every inch of his naked chest gliding against her body, warming her from the inside out. Milly waited until he was over her before she fused her lips to his and urged him onto his back.

Without hesitation, Milly released his mouth and grazed his skin with her lips, working her way down. She teased him the same way he had teased her. Then, with his help, his shorts were removed and her eyes darted to his glorious cock. It was long, thick, and...

Milly looked up at him and smiled. "You're pierced."

AJ slid his hands beneath his head and glanced down his body at her. "You sound pleased."

"You have absolutely no idea how much."

Three

VACATION FLING, ANYONE?

MILLY WAS GOING to drive him fucking crazy.

Ever since she'd pulled his shorts off and noticed the fact that his cock was pierced, she'd been blowing him like it was the only thing in the world she wanted to do.

Her soft, warm mouth drew ragged breaths from him as his balls tightened in anticipation.

"Milly ... baby ... ease up on me."

She lifted her head, those beautiful blue eyes filled with heat and hunger. "Am I hurting you?"

"Not even close," he admitted. "However, I'm not in a race to the finish line."

Rather than lean back down and take his cock in her mouth again, Milly began fisting his length, stroking slowly while her eyes remained locked on his cock. She seemed utterly fascinated by the piercing, which turned him on in a way he'd never imagined.

"Just one more taste?" she asked sweetly, but there wasn't an ounce of sweet in her gaze. She was a vixen ready to pounce.

"Only if I get one, too." He reached for her, pulling her onto him. "You can suck my dick, but I get to lick your pussy."

"I can't find anything wrong with that suggestion," she teased.

"Good, then get on up here and sit on my face."

Her eyes flared, something he'd noticed when he'd mentioned eating her pussy for the first time. Milly enjoyed the dirty talk.

She was breathless as she shifted around so that she was kneeling over his head. AJ didn't waste time, wrapping his arms around her thighs and pulling her down onto his mouth. Milly moaned when he latched onto her clit, grinding down on his face.

He focused on her pleasure. It was working, right up until she put her mouth on his dick again. At that point, his brain went fuzzy. The woman's mouth was a fucking lethal weapon. She was far too good at that.

Somehow, AJ managed to block out the intense feeling of her lips and tongue stroking his dick. He turned his full attention to her pussy, devouring her like a starving man. He worked her, holding her in place when she would've pulled away. He didn't let up until she released his cock from her delectable mouth. Her fingernails dug into his thighs as she screamed, her clit pulsing against his tongue.

Smiling to himself, AJ shifted her onto her side, then he moved around so that he was once again over her, face-to-face.

"You're too good at that," she said with a wide grin. "Way too good."

He chuckled. "Are you ready for the best part?"

Milly was still breathing heavily. "I'm not sure it gets better than that."

"Oh, it does," he promised, pressing his finger against her chest. "Don't go anywhere. I have to grab a condom."

She nodded, watching him when he climbed off the bed.

AJ enjoyed the way she eye-fucked him, her gaze roaming over his entire body as though she couldn't get enough.

When he was walking back to the bed, Milly sat up and changed positions once again, propping her head on a pillow as she stared back at him.

"Spread your legs for me," he insisted, ensuring she saw the heat she evoked in him. "Let me see that pretty pussy."

She inhaled sharply, her knees falling apart, baring the soft pink folds of her pussy. AJ focused on rolling the condom on, never taking his eyes off her.

As he crawled back over her, he rubbed his chest against the smooth flesh between her legs, dragging himself up her body until his mouth found hers again.

Milly kissed him back, her legs wrapping around his hips, holding him in place. He nudged her clit with his cock, sliding through her slick heat.

"AJ," she moaned. "Quit torturing me."

"But I enjoy torturing you," he told her, pushing up with one arm and using his other hand to guide his cock into her slick, welcoming body.

Damn, this woman was killing him. The way she smiled, moaned, even laughed. She was so lighthearted it melted him. AJ wanted to spend the rest of his fucking life buried inside her, doing dirty things to her forever and always.

Okay. And he was letting his thoughts get away from him. He wasn't the type to look forward to tomorrow when it came to his sexual encounters. He generally kept them casual. However, with Milly, he was already looking forward to tomorrow and the day after and…

"AJ," Milly hissed, reaching up and wrapping her arms around his neck.

"Yes, beautiful?"

"Fuck. Me." She added a smile after the rough command, but he knew she was serious.

"You want more?"

"So much more." Milly tried to rock her hips as though she was proving her point.

AJ gave in, sliding in deep, then grinding against her so that his pelvis pressed against her clit.

Milly's eyes rolled back in her head and she moaned softly. "Just. Like. That."

AJ retreated and her eyes shot open. He smiled down at her.

"You're a very mean man, Aaron James Ballard."

He chuckled, then drove in deep and hard.

Milly screamed, her nails digging into his back.

"Is that what you wanted?"

"Yes."

He did it again.

"And don't you dare stop," she commanded.

This woman was amazing. She was funny, smart, sassy. Not to mention, so fucking beautiful it hurt to look at her. He liked that she didn't take too many things seriously, although he could tell by the way she interacted with her friends that she had a heart of gold and would move heaven and earth for those in her inner circle.

Suddenly, AJ wanted to be the center of that circle.

Leaning down, AJ pressed his lips to hers. "Hold on to me, beautiful. Because I'm about to make you scream."

"Don't make promises you can't keep, cowboy," she said with a grin. Her arms tightened around his neck, her legs around his hips.

"Never, baby. And you're about to learn that firsthand." With that, AJ proceeded to show her.

Twice.

*

MILLY WOKE UP the next morning cuddled up to AJ. Before opening her eyes, she took stock of a couple of things. Namely her emotions and her physical state.

Her body ached in the most delicious way, thanks to AJ's phenomenal skills in the sack. Her mind, on the other hand, was slightly off-kilter. She felt as though she'd been thrown from a moving vehicle, then hit by a truck, and now she had to figure out which way was up.

Admittedly, Milly didn't usually have a lot of morning-after emotions. She prepared herself to be disappointed, and she usually was.

"Mornin', beautiful," AJ whispered, pulling her in tighter to his body.

Disappointment was not what she was thinking right then.

"Morning." She sighed, realizing she was far too content. Throwing AJ out of her room wasn't something she was even considering, although it probably should've been.

"Mmm." Milly felt the hard length of AJ's divine cock pressing against her ass. "You're rather excited to see me this morning."

AJ chuckled. "More than you know."

She stiffened in his arms, then prayed he hadn't noticed. Milly was enjoying the casualness of this thing she and AJ had. She would be lying if she said she didn't want to explore it more in depth during their remaining time on the ship. But she had to remember to keep her guard up. There was something about AJ Ballard that got under her skin. And the last thing she wanted was to walk away from this with a broken heart.

"So, what do you say—" Whatever AJ was about to ask was cut off by someone knocking on her cabin door.

Grabbing the sheet, Milly tugged it from the bed and draped it around her before she padded over to see who was there. She opened it enough to peek out, smiling when she noticed her stepbrother standing in the hallway.

"Good morning," Noah greeted, a wide grin on his face.

Not at all embarrassed that her stepbrother had caught her with her hand in the cookie jar so to speak, Milly smiled back. "I hope you're here to bring me breakfast."

"I can. I was just going down to get something for Dare."

Really? That sounded promising. Looked as though her plan to hook Dare and Noah up had worked.

Realizing AJ was still watching her from the bed, Milly hugged the sheet closer to her chest. She lifted one eyebrow, hoping Noah would get on with it.

Noah leaned close, his voice low when he said, "Is someone in there with you?"

She might've blushed just a little. "Maybe."

"Do I even want to know?"

"Probably not."

"Do you want me to bring you breakfast? For two?"

Milly glanced over her shoulder at the sexy, naked man in her bed. "No, I think we're good. Thanks, though."

"I would say be good, but I think that's no longer an option."

Milly giggled. "I'd have to agree with you." She couldn't even bring herself to be embarrassed that she had shagged the sexy bad boy last night. "Oh, and for the record, I no longer need to see Cam's pierced penis. I now have a firsthand experience under my belt."

Noah's eyes widened as though he could've lived the rest of his life without hearing that. Milly laughed, then closed the door. She turned back to AJ.

"Firsthand experience, huh?" he teased.

"Yep. But I'm not sure I had enough time checking out that piercing last night."

"Yeah?"

The man's body was a temple. One she wanted to worship at for the rest of the trip. Of course, it would have to end there, but until then, why couldn't she have a little fun?

Later that night...

MILLY SAT BESIDE AJ while they watched a movie under the stars. About fifteen feet in front of her, she noticed Dare and Noah were doing the same. At first she'd been surprised to see them there, had even been tempted to go join them, but she'd decided against it when she'd seen Noah take Dare's hand.

Although she had stuck her nose where it didn't belong when it came to Gannon and Cam, Milly knew she couldn't do the same with these two. Then again, based on how cozy they were, she probably didn't need to. Her talk with Noah yesterday had been enlightening—probably for him as much as for her. No doubt in her mind, the man had feelings for Dare.

For a brief moment, she wondered what that felt like. To be reunited with someone from your past, someone who'd left such a huge mark on your life...

She dared a glance at AJ and smiled to herself.

Last night, they'd had a few too many drinks and things had happened. This morning, when she'd awoken to find him still in her bed, she'd been a little surprised. But it had been a good surprise.

Granted, she absolutely did not see this going anywhere at all, despite how much she had enjoyed his pierced penis. But it hadn't all been about mind-blowing orgasms. They'd had plenty to talk about, because oddly they had a lot in common, but Milly continued to keep her heart guarded. She knew there was no long term where AJ was concerned. He was a good guy, a gentleman. He had a full-time job, a house, and from their conversations, he had aspirations.

Those were qualities that men who were looking for long term with her tended to lack, and she'd learned to deal with that over the years. In essence, AJ was too much of a grown-up for her, and there was no reason she was going to get her hopes up.

So, she'd passively suggested they enjoy their time together while they were on the ship, making light of any kind of future. For a brief instant, she'd thought she'd seen a little regret in AJ's eyes, but she didn't know him well enough to be sure.

Not that it mattered. Her focus wasn't on herself and she didn't plan for it to be. They had two more days before Gannon and Cam tied the knot, and truth be told, she simply wanted to get to that day. She wanted to watch her best friend marry the love of his life. It made her heart swell to think of the love those two men shared for one another.

She peeked over at AJ once more.

Maybe one day she would be lucky enough to find that.

But she definitely wasn't holding her breath.

Four

TIME TO SAY GOODBYE

IT WAS THE last day of the cruise and AJ wasn't ready for it to be over. He'd spent every night in Milly's bed, hours inside her luscious body, and the mere thought of having to go back to his mundane life didn't sit well with him.

Every minute that Milly wasn't engrossed in taking care of things for the wedding, as well as the wedding itself, AJ had found a way to slip into her sights, ensuring they had more time together. And they were having a good time. Granted, a lot of that was naked time, but so what. Both parties were willing, so he didn't see an issue with that.

Unfortunately, wishful thinking only went so far, because AJ could already feel Milly pulling away. She wasn't distant exactly, but she was certainly more uptight than previous days. He wanted to think she didn't like the idea of going back to shore and separating from him, but he wasn't sure that was the case.

However, he wasn't about to dwell on it, because that would ruin what little time they did have left.

After checking in with Hudson, AJ went in search of Milly. He found her on the upper deck, staring out over the inky-black water. The moon was up, offering more than enough light to see by and AJ took a moment to look his fill. Milly was one of the most beautiful women he'd ever laid eyes on. Long blond hair, bright blue eyes, a rocking body that she outfitted to highlight every phenomenal asset. But AJ knew it wasn't only her outward appearance but also the warm heart and sassy sense of humor that made her the whole package.

He took a chance and moved up behind her, closing her in between his body and the rail.

"What're you doin' out here all alone?" he whispered when he leaned in close to her ear.

He inhaled her, intoxicated by her sweet, fresh scent. He wasn't sure if it was her hair or her perfume, but he loved the way she smelled.

"Just enjoying what's left of the trip."

"The hard part's over, huh?"

Milly leaned back against him. "It is. And I'm tired."

"I can imagine." She had been going nonstop since the first afternoon he'd seen her. They hadn't gotten much sleep at night and then she was always right back up in the morning, moving a million miles a minute.

Milly turned her head back to look up at him. "It's our last night. What do you say we make the most of it?"

"What'd you have in mind?"

She turned in his arms, smiling up at him. "Well, I was thinking we could get naked, then maybe take a shower."

"Hmm." AJ couldn't come up with a single argument. "I could probably be coerced into getting wet."

Milly chuckled, then pulled back and took his hand.

A few minutes later, they slipped into her cabin, and the moment the door closed, AJ pressed her up against the wall, slamming his lips to hers. He wasn't sure what the urgency was, but he felt as though he had to make the most of this time with her.

Milly's arms slipped around his neck as she held on to him, her tongue working his with the same eagerness AJ felt churning in his veins.

It didn't take long before they were both undressed, still standing near the door. He'd had the forethought to grab a condom before he discarded his shorts. Within seconds, he was sheathed. He hefted her up so that her legs wrapped around him. Without prolonging the torture any longer than necessary, AJ aligned their bodies and helped her sink down on him.

A deep, guttural growl escaped him when the warmth of her pussy enveloped his cock. She was so hot, so wet, and the pure pleasure she brought him was something he would never forget.

He broke the kiss and stared into her eyes as he drove deep inside her. He wanted her to feel him. Not just his cock, but all of him. There was something between them that couldn't be denied. Sure, it could've merely been phenomenal sex, but AJ didn't think so.

"Fuck, Milly," he moaned as her inner muscles locked around him. "You feel so good. So perfect."

Milly bucked against him, trying to take him deeper. Standing up wasn't the easiest position to be in, but he didn't want to move, didn't want to dislodge from her body for even a second.

He caught sight of the low dresser in his peripheral vision and came up with a plan. He took the few steps required to get to it before resting her ass on the top. Bracketing her body with his arms, AJ plunged deeper, then withdrew slowly. Minutes passed as he fucked her, their eyes locked as their combined moans and sighs filled the room.

Reaching between them, AJ found her clit with his thumb. He worked her into a frenzy as he continued to slide in and out of her pussy, his cock so fucking hard he hurt. He was past the point of delirium, completely drunk on this woman.

"AJ!" Milly's nails dug into his arms as she held on to him. "I'm … gonna…" Her head tipped back as she screamed.

The sound shot straight to his balls, igniting his release. It barreled through him in a punishing rush, drawing a ragged groan from his throat as he succumbed to the brutality of it.

He kept his eyes locked on her face as he fought to get air into his overworked lungs. He wanted to tell her he had every intention of seeing her once they were back in Texas, but he didn't. The words wouldn't come.

Instead, he smiled. "You mentioned a shower?"

Her answering grin was radiant. "I did."

"I say we get that out of the way and do that again."

Milly chuckled. "I could probably be persuaded to get wet."

Damn.

This woman was something else.

*

The next day

MILLY WOKE EARLY, slipping out of bed while AJ was still asleep. She spent some time on the balcony, letting the warm breeze wash over her as she fought the urge to do something completely insane.

This past week had been amazing. More so because she'd spent every night with AJ in her bed, curled up around her, making her feel safe. Which was the biggest problem. Milly knew deep down no man was capable of making her feel safe. Her personal experience left her weary of all men, especially the bad-boy types who could rock a woman's body in the bedroom. Generally, they were useless outside of it.

On the other hand, Milly wanted nothing more than to tell AJ how she felt, to admit that she would like to see him again once they were back home. In her fantasy, AJ would take her words with relief and agree that they should continue to see each other once they were back in the real world.

However, Milly knew she wouldn't tell him and he wouldn't reciprocate. She'd long ago stopped setting herself up for failure. This had been a vacation fling. An affair that would end as soon as they were on dry land. That was how it was supposed to work, right? They had enjoyed the time they had and any attempt to extend it would only ruin the phenomenal memories of the past few days.

Milly didn't want to cause any issues. Considering AJ was Hudson's brother and she would likely have to see him in the future at some point, she knew she had to end this on good terms. No sense dragging it out until she ended up with a broken heart. At that point, they would part on bad terms, which would ultimately cause problems for her friends. That was the last thing she wanted.

As every second passed, getting them closer and closer to the end of the trip, Milly felt her heart squeeze. It was as though there was a band around it, the real world in control, making it harder and harder to breathe as it tightened.

But she had to look at this rationally. It wasn't like she'd gone and fallen in love with AJ. That wasn't possible. They'd only spent a few days together. Even if the sex was incredible, that didn't mean it would result in a happy every after.

That was the same thing she told herself with every guy she encountered. And there had been many. Not that she was entirely proud of that, but Milly wasn't a prude. She knew what she wanted, and although she never got it, that hadn't stopped her from trying.

In the past.

The new Milly—the smart, adult version—wasn't naive enough to believe that great sex led to a relationship.

That didn't mean she and AJ couldn't be friends. She would be cordial to him. Maybe one day they'd be able to attend a function at the same time. Perhaps something at the marina. If she could put some space between them now, it would reduce the risk of things being awkward in the future.

She heard the sound of the door opening behind her and her heart skipped a beat.

"Good morning," AJ greeted when he moved up behind her.

Milly turned in his arms and smiled up at his handsome, sleepy face. "Good morning. Looks like it's back to dry land for us today."

His gaze slid to the horizon and she knew he could see it the same as she could. The trip was over, they would be leaving the ship within a couple of hours, and all of this would become a pleasant memory.

Standing on tiptoe, Milly kissed his scruffy cheek. "I have to start packing my stuff." She smiled brightly. "You probably should, too."

AJ's beautiful green eyes met hers. "Yeah. I guess so."

Not wanting to prolong the inevitable, Milly slid around him and headed back into the cabin.

"Milly."

She didn't turn around to look at him. She couldn't. If she did, she feared she would waver. Since that was the worst idea in the world, Milly kept her attention on the door, her hand on the knob. "Hmm?"

"I…" AJ sighed heavily. "I had a great time."

Ignoring her heart, Milly glanced over her shoulder. "Me, too."

More than he would ever know.

Five

CRICKETS...

Three weeks later, June

SITTING IN THE airport terminal, AJ glanced at his phone screen. Well, glared was a more apt description. He wanted to incinerate the damn thing with his eyeballs and pretend the phone was at fault for Milly not responding to him for the past three weeks.

Not once since they returned to shore had Milly answered any of his texts or his phone calls.

He hit the button to pull up the text message thread that he'd been adding to day after day. He scrolled up to the first one, sent the night they had gotten back to Texas.

Hey, just checking in. Wanted to make sure you got home all right.

No response.

Hey, Mill. Wondered if maybe you wanted to grab a drink this week. Perhaps dinner.

Not a peep.

It's been a week since we got back, just thought I'd check on you. Hope everything's okay.

Nothing.

All right. Now I'm starting to worry, Milly. Can you please just text me back so I know you're all right?

Evidently she couldn't, because she hadn't.

There were several more, all reflecting how completely ridiculous he was. He looked like a love-struck kid, eager to catch the attention of his crush. It seemed AJ was the only one who remembered those nights they'd spent together.

His thoughts drifted back to the first conversation they'd had. When she had discreetly probed as to the status of his relationship, he had done the same to her. Her response: I'm the kinda girl who ends up with the bad boy, and while it's fun to entertain them, they're always looking for the next best thing.

Fun to entertain them, huh? Was that what he was to her? The bad boy who she believed was ready to move on to the next best thing? Surely he hadn't given her that impression, had he?

AJ sighed and considered sending her another message, but he shook off the thought. He already looked far more desperate than he was comfortable with.

After it became apparent Milly wouldn't text him back, AJ had commenced with calling her. He left stupid voicemails. A few words, nothing serious. While the anger churned inside, he had masked it, asking her to call him.

Three long weeks he'd been acting like a fool. And for three long weeks, Milly had ignored him.

AJ knew it was time to move on. He had no choice but to put her in the past and get with the program. He had a job that needed his full attention. He was about to walk onto a plane. Another trip to California was on the agenda. He had clients to see, asses to kiss, bigwigs to schmooze. He didn't have time to be chasing Milly. Even if he did, it was obvious she didn't want to be caught.

Later that evening, AJ sat in the hotel bar. He'd frequented this place over the past five years or so. It wasn't his favorite place to be, but it offered a bit of solace from his thoughts. It was always busy with mostly business professionals staying there. This particular hotel was one the local companies utilized for their out-of-town guests.

As he sat staring at a rum and Coke, he fought the urge to drink it. AJ knew he didn't have a problem with alcohol, but he'd gone on the straight and narrow years ago when it became obvious he was quickly heading in that direction. So, rather than end up with an addiction he couldn't get out from under, he'd stopped drinking altogether.

Now, he wanted that drink more than anything else.

Well, maybe not anything. He would've preferred Milly; however, she clearly wasn't on the menu.

"Someone sitting here?"

AJ glanced over at the woman with the sweet, feminine voice. A smile tilted his lips when he recognized the familiar face. He motioned for her to have a seat.

"Fancy meeting you here," Sue said with a smile, her glossy lips curled upward.

"I didn't realize you were visiting this side of the country these days." AJ fingered the glass as he stared at the beautiful brunette now sitting beside him.

"It looks as though I'll be back for a while," Sue admitted.

AJ liked Sue. They'd spent quite a bit of time together in the past, a lot of it naked in her room or his. Sue had been quite the treat back when he found himself lonely. They'd hooked up repeatedly, agreeing from the beginning that nothing serious would ever come from their out-of-town rendezvous. So, with those terms in mind, they'd thoroughly enjoyed one another.

He knew it wouldn't take much to convince her to take her drink up to his room so they could engage in a one-nighter. She wasn't the clingy type, which AJ approved of. However, as he glanced over her from head to toe, he knew he wasn't going to suggest anything of the sort. He had no desire to bed her regardless of how willing she might be.

Then again, he was getting ahead of himself. It was quite possible Sue was in a relationship. He hadn't seen her in almost a year. Hell, she could be married with a kid at home if she'd found someone who struck her fancy.

The bartender appeared to take Sue's drink order.

"White wine, thank you."

He disappeared quickly.

"So, how're things?" she probed, turning slightly so that she was facing him.

Her body language was open, inviting. AJ glanced down at her ring finger. There was no sparkling rock signifying that she'd drifted into wedded bliss.

"Good," he told her, turning his drink, debating on whether or not he would down it and risk giving in to his male impulses.

His thoughts drifted to Milly, to their time on the ship. He fucking missed her and it was killing him. He hated that she was ignoring him when the only thing he wanted was to spend more time with her. Didn't necessarily have to be naked time, either. They'd passed a lot of hours laughing and joking, getting to know one another.

But he was the discardable bad boy. That was what he'd determined after hours of thinking about it. She had entertained him for those few days, never considering something might come out of it. She'd had her mind made up in the very beginning.

"Earth to AJ," Sue said, snapping her fingers.

When he focused on her, he noticed her smiling. AJ briefly wondered if Sue felt the same. Was he the bad boy she wanted to use and discard? Was he that to all the women he'd spent time with over the years?

"Penny for your thoughts."

AJ shook his head. "Just work shit," he lied as he glanced down at his watch. "In fact, I really should head up to my room. I've got a presentation to work on."

Sue's brown eyes glittered. "Is that an invitation?"

AJ pushed off the stool and tossed a twenty on the bar. "Not tonight." He offered a wicked grin. "But maybe I'll catch you tomorrow."

"I'll be here."

Which meant AJ wouldn't.

As angry as he was at Milly, the mere thought of spending the night with another woman only pissed him off more.

*

THE INSTANT GANNON opened his front door, Milly practically threw herself into his arms.

"Well, nice to see you, too," he said with a chuckle.

"I missed you so much." She squeezed him tightly. "I've been counting down the days until you got back from your honeymoon."

It was true.

Granted, she had given him a few days to acclimate before she barged back into his world, but enough was enough. Milly needed someone to talk to and her best friend was the only person who would understand what she was going through.

"Well, come in," he urged, placing his hand on her back and gently nudging her into the house.

"Where's Cam?"

"At the marina. Busy time for them right now."

Milly could only imagine. Summertime at the marina was hectic. She'd seen it firsthand. And for Cam to have been gone, that had to be tough. He handled most of the business end, which meant he would have plenty to keep him busy.

"Can I get you something to drink? Wine? Water? Tea?"

Normally, Milly would jump at the opportunity for wine, but … well, that wasn't a good idea right now.

"Tea sounds perfect," she told him.

Gannon's eyes narrowed as he studied her. "Is something wrong?"

"No," she huffed. "Why?"

"Because I'm not sure you've ever turned down wine."

Milly waved him off. "Oh, hush. It's too hot for wine. Plus, I'm driving."

"Right." Gannon stared at her for another moment before turning toward the kitchen.

Milly followed, setting her purse on the table by the door. She squared her shoulders and put on a brave face.

"So, how was it?"

"How was what?" Gannon poured two glasses of tea.

"Really? You're going there?"

Gannon smirked. "It was amazing, Mill."

Of course it was. Their honeymoon was probably full of fun days and sleepless nights. Not that Milly was jealous.

Okay, maybe she was a little jealous. After all, Gannon had fallen in love and he was living his happy ever after.

Did it make her a bad person to want that?

"What about you?" Gannon asked, bringing over two tea glasses and setting them on the kitchen table.

Milly frowned, not understanding his question.

"I happen to know you and AJ were hot and heavy on the cruise. How's it been since you came back?"

She waved him off. "That was a vacation fling. It's over now."

"Really?" Gannon didn't look convinced. "Why's that? He ignoring you?"

Milly stared into her glass, hoping the question would simply vanish into thin air. She honestly didn't want to talk about AJ.

Okay, fine. That was a big fat lie. She wanted to talk about AJ. In fact, she wanted to talk to AJ. But she'd already spent the past few weeks ignoring him and now she felt like an idiot. She hadn't heard from him in a couple of days, which meant he had likely moved on to someone else.

"Milly…"

Her eyes cut to Gannon, who was staring at her expectantly.

"No, he's not ignoring me. I'm ignoring him," she admitted.

"Why? He suck in bed?"

Her face heated. Although Gannon was her very best friend in the whole wide world, Milly still had a hard time talking about certain things with him. Such as how a guy was in bed.

Granted, she liked giving Cam and Gannon a hard time and she didn't shy away from much, but when it came to this—discussing the exquisite way AJ had played her body—Milly couldn't find the words.

Gannon cleared his throat, evidently waiting for an answer.

Milly stared back at him and grinned. "He was great in bed," she finally admitted.

"Okay, so what's the problem?"

Shrugging, Milly dropped her gaze to the table. "I know how it works, Gannon. We might've spent a few hours doing the horizontal mambo, but eventually, it would've gotten old and AJ would've kicked me to the curb. At that point, it would've been weird for everyone involved. I'm simply fast-forwarding things and omitting the part where I fall in love with the man and end up getting my heart broken."

Gannon's hand landed on her forearm. A soft, gentle touch that had tears springing to her eyes. Her stupid emotions had been rioting these past few weeks. It seemed no matter how hard she tried, they were overwhelming her and she didn't like it one bit.

"Mill. Look at me."

She forced her gaze to meet his.

"You can't predict the future, no matter how hard you try. And pushing AJ away isn't going to stop you from having feelings for him."

"I don't have feelings for him," she argued. If she did, she didn't want to, anyway.

"Really?" He didn't appear convinced. "Because you sure do look miserable."

"I've been sick," she admitted. "I haven't been feeling well."

His dark eyebrow raised. "What's wrong?"

She shook her head. "No idea."

That was a lie. Milly suspected she knew what was wrong, but she couldn't quite wrap her head around it. And until she did that, she was keeping her suspicions to herself.

"Well, honey, I really hope you'll talk to me. You know I'm here for you, no matter what."

Milly smiled sadly. "I know. And I'm fine. Really." She reached for her glass. "Now seriously. Let's talk about you. Tell me all about the honeymoon."

Gannon groaned.

Clearly, her best friend wasn't happy that he was going to be the topic of conversation.

Six

A SHOW OF SOLIDARITY

Seven weeks later, August

AJ STARED AT the television screen, but he wasn't seeing much of the baseball game he was watching with his brother. Even the quiet night in wasn't helping to ease the strain in AJ's brain.

No matter how hard he tried, he couldn't stop thinking about Milly. She had not answered any of his messages, so he'd given up trying. For the past few weeks, he'd had to hide his damn phone from himself so he wouldn't risk sending her a stupid text asking for her to talk to him.

Not once in his entire life had AJ been so fucking lovestruck over a woman. But that seemed to be exactly what he was. He thought of Milly every single day. When he took a shower, he remembered the showers they'd taken together. When he ate dinner, he thought about sharing meals with her. When he had a beer, he thought about the times they'd spent on the ship talking about everything and nothing at all.

Needless to say, the past eleven weeks since he'd left that ship had been the worst that he could recall. AJ just fucking wanted to hear her voice, to see her, to listen to her laugh.

He was pathetic.

Hudson's phone buzzed, drawing AJ out of his stupor. He glanced over at his brother as he pulled his phone from his pocket. His expression went from relaxed to stressed in under a second.

"What's up?" AJ asked, curious.

Teague, Hudson signed.

"Something wrong?"

Hudson shrugged but pushed to his feet.

"Where're you going?"

Hudson signed, I have to go to the marina.

"I'll go with you," AJ offered, not sure what he was walking into but it was rare for his brother to panic. And this was definitely panic.

Without waiting for him, Hudson grabbed his keys and headed for the door. AJ did the same, grabbing his truck keys and chasing after him.

"What's going on with him?" AJ hollered as he raced toward his truck.

Hudson shrugged again.

Well, shit.

"I'll see you there," AJ yelled before jumping into his truck.

He wasn't sure he'd ever seen Hudson this upset before. Then again, he wasn't sure he'd ever seen his brother quite so taken with a man, either. And despite what Hudson wanted everyone to believe, AJ knew his brother was in deep when it came to Teague.

AJ didn't know a lot about the kid, other than he had some issues. Something or someone had hurt Teague and he walked around with a huge chip on his shoulder.

When Hudson laid rubber to asphalt in front of AJ's house, he knew something was seriously wrong. He put his foot to the floor and followed him.

Fifteen minutes later, he was pulling into the parking lot behind Hudson. He noticed there were several other vehicles already there and a handful of people standing around. He put the truck in park, then climbed out.

As he walked over, AJ scanned the many faces before him. Cam, Gannon, Dare, Noah, Roan, along with Cam's father and a man AJ didn't recognize were standing in a huddle.

"You have any idea what's wrong with Teague?" Cam asked Hudson directly.

Hudson shook his head.

"Something going on with you two?" Unlike Cam, who sounded concerned, Roan's tone held a bit of accusation.

Hudson stared Roan down, but he didn't respond. Instead, he pulled out his phone. AJ assumed he was texting

Teague, likely trying to figure out where he was and what he was doing. Once he put his phone back in his pocket, Hudson turned to Roan and signed: Where did he go?

Roan shrugged. "He didn't say. But he was pissed. More so than I've ever seen him."

AJ moved closer. "Does he have any family? Maybe he went there."

Cam shook his head. "Not that we know of."

"Did he put an emergency contact down on his application when you hired him?" AJ asked.

Cam grinned. "Yeah. Nine-one-one."

"Well, that doesn't help."

Before they could brainstorm any more, Cam's father's phone rang. He answered immediately. Everyone stood there watching him as he spoke calmly to whoever the caller was. When he hung up, he directed his attention to the group.

"A woman just called in to emergency dispatch. Apparently, there's a blond guy sitting on her private pier."

"Shit," Roan snarled.

Text me the address, Hudson signed to Cam.

"Will do."

Hudson spun around and raced back to his truck, everyone else following.

Ten minutes later, AJ slammed his truck into park once more and jumped out. His brother took off like a shot across private yards, racing toward the lake. AJ followed in hot pursuit, his chest aching at the thought of something happening to Teague. AJ knew Hudson would never forgive himself if that happened.

AJ noticed Hudson throwing things out of his pockets before he dove into the water, disappearing into the inky darkness.

Holding his breath, AJ shot up a silent prayer. Please let Teague be all right. Please let him be all right.

Time stood still as AJ waited for Hudson to emerge from the water. He started to panic, wondering if he should go in after his brother. Suddenly, Hudson appeared, hefting Teague's dead weight.

AJ threw himself to the wooden planks of the pier and reached over the side, wrapping his arms around Teague and lifting him out of the water.

Once the man was laid out flat, AJ put two fingers against Teague's neck, then looked at Hudson. "Fuck. I don't know CPR."

His heart raced. How the fuck was he supposed to help?

As soon as Hudson was out of the water, he dropped to his knees beside Teague. He started the process of CPR while AJ dialed 911.

When the operator answered, AJ frantically relayed the details of what had happened. They'd found a man in the water; he was unconscious. That was basically all he knew. "Yes, we need an ambulance."

Minutes felt like days as Hudson pressed on Teague's chest, attempting to make his heart work. Finally, Teague started choking, spurting water. AJ released the breath he hadn't realized he'd been holding as Hudson flipped Teague onto his side, allowing him to expel the lake water.

AJ breathed a sigh of relief. Another came close on the heels of that one when the EMTs arrived to take over the difficult task of ensuring Teague stayed alive.

How the hell had this happened? What was Teague doing? More importantly, why? Had he tried to commit suicide? AJ suspected it, but he didn't want to voice it, certainly not to Hudson.

Hudson was shaking like a leaf as AJ pulled him out of the chaos, allowing the professionals to take over. He steered Hudson along until he saw Cam standing nearby.

AJ watched his brother as Hudson turned to Cam and Dare, the two people who knew Teague better than anyone else.

When Roan appeared a second later, Hudson's hands started working: He needs help. Hudson nodded toward the water. Professional help. He tried to kill himself. I don't know about you, but I am not willing to lose him.

Fucking hell. AJ had been hoping it was anything but that.

"I agree," Cam said softly, his eyes searching Hudson's face.

AJ stood there feeling useless. He didn't know the first thing about Teague, other than the fact that Hudson obviously cared about him. As did the others. Teague was important to them, there was no doubt about that. They were a tight-knit group and AJ admired that about them.

"Think he'll listen?" Dare asked.

"Don't think he'll have much of a choice," Roan stated somberly.

Hudson signed: I'm going home to change, then I'm going to the hospital.

Roan nodded. "We'll meet you there and we'll talk more about this then. But I think we're all on the same page. He tried to take his own life. Next time, we might not be there to save him."

Knowing his brother was going to need as much support as he could get, AJ decided to go with him.

*

WHEN GANNON CALLED to tell her they'd found Teague, Milly broke down into tears. She had already gotten dressed to go searching the local clubs, eager to offer whatever help she could.

Thankfully, her help wasn't needed, because they had found Teague. According to Gannon, he wasn't doing well, but at least he was alive.

It took roughly fifteen minutes to pull herself together when she got the news. Once she did that, she went to the bathroom and washed her face before pulling her hair back into a ponytail. She looked like a woman who had been crying her eyes out for the past couple of hours. In all fairness, she had been. Plus, Milly was going to the hospital. She didn't need to be all dolled up to do that because it really didn't matter what she looked like.

An hour later, Milly was sitting in the hospital waiting room with Cam, Gannon, Roan, and AJ. Dare had gone back with Hudson to talk to Teague. Apparently, Dare was going to translate Hudson's sign language so Teague would understand.

Milly knew that everyone who worked at the marina was learning sign language so they could eliminate the communication barrier with Hudson. It had been Dare's idea, actually, and everyone else had jumped on board. While she didn't know much, Milly had been getting a few lessons from Dare here and there.

"I still can't believe he did this," Cam said, thrusting his hands in his hair. "Why didn't he come to us for help?"

Milly wasn't sure who he was talking to. Gannon was the one to respond, but only by putting his hand on Cam's back. A silent reassurance that he understood his pain.

This was the hardest thing she'd had to do as of late. Watching her friends hurting, knowing Teague was in even more pain. He had to be, right? To attempt to take his own life. She wanted to hug him, to tell him it would all be all right.

Granted, she didn't know that was the case, because she didn't know how to help him.

Her gaze cut to AJ.

This was the first time she'd seen him since the cruise. He looked good. Healthy, handsome. She wanted to curl up in his arms and cry. To feel safe for a little while. He'd made her feel that way on the cruise.

But she had ruined her chances with him by ignoring him, which meant she had to keep her distance. Thankfully, he hadn't tried to talk to her. She wasn't sure what she would even say to him. Apologize, maybe? For being an asshole?

His green eyes lifted and met her gaze. Milly sucked in air. He was a shock to her system. She could see the pain in his eyes, but she wasn't sure if it was from her or the situation his brother currently found himself in. According to Gannon, AJ had been there to help pull Teague out of the water.

Her chest ached, the need to break down almost too much to ignore. She wanted to cry.

It was hormones, she knew. Although she hadn't been to the doctor to confirm, Milly had missed two periods, which had prompted her to take a pregnancy test. According to the little plastic stick and those glaring blue lines, she was pregnant. Only, she wasn't sure she believed it. And what would AJ say when she told him? He would likely tell her she was crazy. He would want proof, no doubt. Even though she hadn't slept with anyone else for months before him and certainly no one after, she wouldn't blame him for wanting her to prove it.

Except, Milly hadn't told anyone. Not even Gannon.

She knew she would have to soon because she wouldn't be able to hide it forever. Right now she wasn't showing, but she could practically feel the baby growing inside her.

Milly was jerked from her thoughts when Dare appeared. He was alone, which meant Hudson was still with Teague.

The men got to their feet and walked over to him. Milly remained seated, needing to get her emotions under control. Her eyes strayed to AJ once more. His back was to her. His strong, muscular back. Those wide shoulders. The man would be able to take on her burden and probably help her through this.

If only she was strong enough to tell him.

Not yet. Not until you go to the doctor.

Milly wanted to be absolutely certain. The doctor would be able to tell her a due date, although, based on the math, she had already figured March. But that was important information to have. So, until she did that, she was going to keep her secret. From everyone.

When Hudson emerged from the mouth of the hallway a short time later, Milly forced herself to her feet.

Hudson started to sign and Dare translated for everyone who didn't understand. Something about getting Teague checked into a hospital. One that would help him deal with his depression in a healthy way. That way he didn't down a fifth of whiskey and end up at the bottom of a lake again.

Milly sobbed when she thought about Teague under the water, his life draining out of him. How could he not see how much they all cared about him? How much life he brought to their little family? He was an important piece and it broke her heart to think he didn't realize that.

AJ turned to her and the next thing Milly knew, she was in his arms, her nose pressed against his chest. She let herself go in that moment, crying in earnest. Heartbroken for Teague. She wished she knew how to help him, but she didn't.

She heard the others still talking, but she didn't let go of AJ.

"Inpatient or outpatient?" Roan asked.

There was silence for a moment before Dare spoke. "He says outpatient, but we'll let him make that decision when he gets there."

Obviously those were Hudson's words.

"Agreed," Cam stated. "They have a partial inpatient program also. I've already contacted them, and they'll gladly take him as a patient, either way. He'll need to be evaluated by their doctors."

Whatever Teague decided, Milly only hoped it was the right choice for him.

She was quickly learning that although they seemed right at the time, not all choices were for the best.

Certainly not in her case.

Seven

A HAPPY ACCIDENT

Five weeks later, September

AJ PACED HIS living room.

Aside from the night in the hospital, AJ hadn't heard from Milly. Not until roughly two hours ago when she texted him and asked if she could come over.

He'd been so shocked, he had instantly responded with, sure. Now he couldn't stop thinking about what she wanted to talk about. Was she wanting to apologize for ignoring him for the past three months? Maybe seeing him at the hospital had brought back good memories? Did she want to give this thing between them a chance? After all this time?

It seemed odd if she did. Still, Milly could've easily texted him with that. She didn't need a face-to-face to get that off her chest. Either way, he would've accepted her apology and then proceeded to ask her out again.

That night at the hospital, when AJ had wrapped his arms around Milly when she started to cry, it had all come back to him. In short, he missed her greatly. He still wasn't willing to move on without getting some closure where she was concerned.

So maybe it was a good thing that she was coming by. Having her face-to-face would mean she couldn't hide from him. However, for the life of him, he couldn't figure out what she could possibly want to talk about.

He growled his frustration, then headed to the kitchen. He could make them lunch. Maybe she would stay and eat. But what did he make? Sandwiches? Soup? Hell, he didn't have much of anything in his house. Most of the time he ordered takeout or delivery.

Perhaps he could order a pizza. What did she like on her pizza?

Before he could work himself into more of a frenzy, his doorbell rang.

AJ spun around and stared at the front door.

That was Milly. She had come over. She wanted to talk.

Answer the door, dumb ass.

Right.

AJ took the advice of that stupid voice in his head and went to the front door. Without looking to see who it was, he opened it quickly and stared down at the most beautiful woman in the world.

Her sunglasses shielded her eyes, but her smile was perfect. "Hey."

AJ swallowed hard. "Hey."

Milly glanced past him, then looked up into his eyes once more. "Can I come in?"

Shit. He was a dumb ass.

Stepping back out of the way, he motioned her inside. He closed the door slowly before turning to face her. Milly was peering around his house as she pushed her sunglasses on top of her head.

"This is nice," she said, sounding somewhat surprised. "Not the bachelor pad I thought it would be."

AJ didn't have much in his house, but what he had was decent. His furniture matched and he'd long ago gotten rid of the mismatched crap he'd had in college. Granted, he didn't spend too much time at home, so it still seemed somewhat sparse.

"Thanks."

Milly turned to face him.

"Can I get you something to drink?"

"I … uh…" Her gaze shot to the floor. "Actually, maybe we should talk first. And if you decide not to throw me out, we can discuss the drink."

AJ frowned. Why the hell would he throw her out of his house?

Gotta talk to find that out.

Since it was obvious she wanted to get right to the point, AJ motioned toward the sofa before he took a seat on the other.

He'd never been the type to get tongue-tied, yet that was how he found himself with Milly.

"So…" She sat on the edge of the cushion, as though she intended to bolt at any moment.

AJ watched her intently, silently urging her to spill it. If she wanted to apologize, he wanted to accept so they could move on. Perhaps he could take her out tonight. It was Monday, but they could still grab something for dinner. He would be going out of town tomorrow, but that didn't matter tonight.

Milly's bright blue eyes locked on his. "I know I've ignored you the past few months, and first of all, I want to apologize for that. It was rude and you deserve better than that. In my defense, I was scared. I'm not good at relationships, and I figured it would be better to not have one than to go through the inevitable heartache."

"Milly—"

She effectively cut him off by holding up her hand. "Hold on. I'm not done."

But he wanted to accept her apology. It was all he cared about.

"That's not why I'm here, AJ."

His hope sank instantly. So much for taking her to dinner.

"I have to just say it or I'll never get it out," she said, her eyes on the wall behind him.

"Okay. Say it."

Those pretty blue eyes snapped to his face and she looked uncertain.

"Whatever it is, I'm sure it's fine, Milly."

She shook her head. "I'm not so sure about that."

"Well, I won't know until you tell me."

Milly nodded. "Fine." She inhaled deeply, let it out slowly. "I'm pregnant."

Pregnant?

AJ's mind went blank. His entire world centered on that single word. He had to assume he was the father, otherwise, she wouldn't be here telling him as much. Right?

"You're not gonna say anything?" She sounded worried.

What was he supposed to say?

"Look," she said quickly. "I'm really sorry. But I thought it was only fair that you know."

"When's the baby due?"

Milly's eyes narrowed. "I assure you this baby's yours, AJ."

He frowned, confused. "I…" AJ inched closer to the edge of the cushion. "I wasn't disputing that. I was curious when the due date is."

"Oh." She looked sincerely perplexed. "March eighth."

AJ didn't bother doing the math. If she believed he was the father, he had no reason to believe otherwise.

"So, that means you're three months along?"

"Four," she corrected. "Sixteen weeks." Her gaze dropped to her belly. When she smoothed out her shirt, he saw the faint impression of a bump. Not much of one at all, but yeah, okay, maybe she would look pregnant if she was naked.

God, he wanted to see her naked.

*

MILLY WASN'T SURE what she'd expected AJ to say or do or even feel when she told him she was pregnant. However, it certainly wasn't for him to sit there as though he wanted to inhale her.

The look in his eyes was primal. It had her body heating. Nothing to worry about. It was a normal reaction to the hottest man on the planet. No need to fret. When she left his house, she could go back to her normal, sexless existence.

Oh, God. She wanted to have sex with AJ. Right here. Right now.

Damn pregnancy hormones.

Milly had to remind herself that she wasn't here to ogle him. She was here to relay the information so he was well aware he was going to be a father. What he did with that information would be up to him.

"AJ?"

"Hmm?"

"Are you going to say anything?"

"So … uh … do we know how this happened?" The second the words were out of AJ's mouth, he looked shocked.

"I mean … I know how babies are made and all that, it's just…"

"We used condoms?" she supplied. "I was thinking about that. Did one of the condoms break, maybe?"

AJ shook his head. "Not that I know of. If I'd even thought so, I would've said something, Milly."

"It's just…" Milly felt her face heat with embarrassment. "I did some research and it said that with a piercing, there's a better chance of the condom ripping. I mean, I don't know for a fact. I'm not pierced or anything, you know."

AJ grinned. "I get it. But no. Not that I could tell, anyway."

She believed him. Not once had she thought this was anything more than an accident. A happy accident. At least for her. The thought of being a mother—while terrifying— filled her with an odd excitement.

"I know you would have," she told him so he didn't worry that she blamed him. "Some things happen for a reason, I guess."

AJ nodded. "Yeah. I guess they do." His green eyes cleared and he was once again focused on her face. "I wanna be a part of the baby's life."

Milly inhaled deeply as the tears threatened to fall. She cried at the drop of a hat these days, so it wasn't unexpected.

"Really?"

"Really." AJ pushed to his feet and joined her on the sofa. He cupped her face. "I'm not the one who was running away from this thing, Milly."

True. But that didn't mean he was ready to be a father. They had used condoms, so this was a fluke. Granted, she wasn't going to come up with excuses, because she had long ago accepted the pregnancy. In fact, from the very second she thought she was pregnant, Milly had known this was meant to be.

"I wanna be part of the pregnancy, too," he whispered. "If you'll let me."

How could she tell him no? She wanted him to be part of it all. Mainly because she was tired of being alone.

Not that she was alone. She had Gannon and Cam and the rest of the marina boys, but she didn't have them the way she wanted AJ.

"So, doctor's appointments?" she asked.

AJ nodded.

"Oh, wait." Milly pulled away and grabbed her purse.

She searched deep until she found the small photo album she'd stuck in there. She pulled it out and opened it before passing it over to AJ.

"That's the first sonogram. I didn't find out for certain until … yesterday."

AJ's eyes darted from her face to the black-and-white picture. He turned it this way and that, likely trying to figure out what it was.

Milly pointed. "That's her head, her rump, and one of her hands."

His head snapped up. "Her?"

Milly smiled. "Well, we don't know for sure just yet. The doctor said she can't tell for certain until twenty weeks, but she said she didn't see a penis … so, I'm calling her a she for now."

For a second, she thought AJ was going to cry. She understood the overwhelming feeling. She'd been there when her doctor shared the news of the baby's sex. Despite the fact it wasn't absolutely certain, Milly had a feeling.

She remained quiet while he stared at the sonogram photo. She watched him, admiring the beautiful lines of his face. God, she'd missed him.

When he finally handed the album back, Milly tucked it into her purse.

"I just want us to be friends, AJ," she said, hoping he would agree to the same.

"Friends?"

Milly nodded.

"I want more than friends, Milly."

This was the hard part, she knew. Milly wasn't sure she was ready for more than friends. She had so much to think about. Namely trying to figure out how to be a mom. She didn't have the slightest idea how to be a parent. She was reading books, trying to educate herself on diapers and feedings. It was all so overwhelming. She didn't think she'd have time for anything else.

"Can we start with friends?" she asked, staring back at him. "I just… I need to get through the pregnancy, AJ. I don't…" She didn't know how to finish that sentence.

AJ's eyes remained locked on her face. He was quiet for the longest time and she sensed some residual pain from her request. Admittedly, Milly'd had a great time with him on the ship. However, she always ended up on the bad side of the relationship and she didn't want that with AJ. He was her child's father. She didn't want anything to come between him and their daughter. Certainly not her.

"We'll take it one day at a time," she added, hoping he would agree.

Finally, AJ nodded. "One day at a time."

Relief swamped her.

"But I want to see you, Milly. I want to spend time with you. Doesn't matter when or where. You just can't shut me out anymore."

He was right. She couldn't. And if they were going to be friends, there was no reason she would have to. They could do this together if they put their minds to it. She didn't have to be alone and clueless. He could be right there with her. They could learn together.

"I won't," she promised. "No more shutting you out."

"Good." AJ flopped back on the sofa, his eyes closing. "I'm gonna be a dad."

The way he said it wasn't negative. His words were laced with wonder. When he opened his eyes and peered over at her, she knew he was feeling the same way she had when she found out. Lost, excited, worried. They were natural emotions, she assumed.

"I didn't grow up with a father," AJ admitted. "He hightailed it when I was little."

Milly frowned.

"I won't know what to do."

Milly's frown flipped as she reached for his hand. "Well, I had a great dad. He's excited, by the way.[1] And regardless, we'll figure it out together."

AJ smiled and squeezed her hand. "I guess that's the plan, then. Let's figure this out together."

Had it really been this easy? When Milly had talked to Gannon, she'd worked herself into a frenzy, terrified about how AJ would take the news. He didn't deny her or the baby. In fact, she'd go so far as to say he was happy about the news.

"Does anyone else know?" he asked. "Other than your dad?"

"Just Gannon. Probably Cam since they're married. I asked him not to say anything until I could tell you."

"Well, I guess it's time to tell the masses, huh?"

"What do you think Hudson will say?" she asked.

"Your guess is as good as mine."

Milly laughed even as tears filled her eyes.

Damn pregnancy hormones.

Eight

TIME FLIES WHEN YOU'RE HAVING FUN

One month later, October

AJ SAT BESIDE Milly on her sofa while they watched Pretty Woman, a movie he never would've picked out if he'd had a choice. Since he left their movie nights up to Milly, he couldn't complain.

For the past few weeks, AJ had been spending as much time with Milly as he could. He would take her to lunch on the weekends when he was in town, and he made a point to text her all the time to see how she was. She was no longer ignoring him and AJ breathed easier because of it.

Milly must've felt him watching her because she peeked over and smiled. Before AJ could smile back, her cell phone rang.

Hitting mute on the television, AJ waited while Milly answered the call.

"Hey, Gannon. You sad you weren't invited to watch Pr—"

She paused and AJ assumed Gannon was saying something. When her eyes widened, her mouth falling open, his heart lurched into his chest. The thought of someone calling to give her bad news wasn't something he wanted to contemplate. As it was, AJ was trying to keep Milly as stress free as possible.

"What do you mean Roan has a baby?" Her voice was pitched high, panic glistening in her eyes. "Cassie's baby?"

AJ didn't know who Cassie was.

"Oh, my God, Gannon! She's dead? How? Why?"

Milly was silent and AJ assumed Gannon was relaying more information.

"Is Roan okay? How's the baby?"

Once again she was silent and AJ kept his eyes on hers.

"Okay. Yeah. Sure. Tell Roan I'm here if he needs me. I'm more than willing to watch the baby if that'll help."

Milly hung up the phone and turned to him.

"That was Gannon. Roan's sister's dead."

"Holy fuck."

"Yeah. I know." Milly's eyes dropped to her belly. "Apparently his sister was an addict. Roan found her in her house with a syringe in her arm."

Fucking hell. "You mentioned a baby?"

"Yes!" Her eyes widened as they met his. "Apparently, Roan's been taking care of his sister's baby. And he didn't bother to tell anyone!"

So much for keeping Milly stress free.

<<>>

Two weeks later, Halloween

AJ sat on his front porch with Milly, waiting for the trick-or-treaters to show up. She had insisted they be there to pass out candy, and since his neighborhood would have more kids than hers, they had decided to come here.

With his heart in his throat, AJ willingly did as Milly requested, enjoying every single second he got to spend with her and, admittedly, falling more and more in love with her every damn day.

<<>>

November

AJ had expected to spend Thanksgiving alone. He would have, too, if Milly hadn't called, insisting that he come to her father's house for the holiday. Apparently, Dare and Noah would be there, as well.

Since he'd already met her father once and the man hadn't pulled a shotgun out of his closet, AJ had agreed.

Needless to say, it had been one of the best Thanksgivings he'd had in a while.

<<>>

December

Christmas was never a big holiday for AJ. Not even before his mother had taken her own life. Having lived with a woman who was so deep in depression, AJ had come to expect her to not want to celebrate much of anything.

So, this year, after he returned from his business trip in California, AJ had expected to come home to an empty house.

He'd been surprised to find Milly there.

"I'm not much of a cook," she admitted. "But I thought maybe we could have a little Christmas dinner of our own."

With that simple request, AJ had fallen completely in love with the woman.

Not that he had told her.

<<>>

January

AJ sat on Milly's sofa, her feet in his lap. He still couldn't believe they'd made it through the past four months since she told him she was pregnant without a single hiccup. Well, not between them, anyway. There had been quite a few road bumps for Roan as of late, but they were trying to pitch in where they could. After all, according to Milly, spending time with Liam was giving them a firsthand glimpse of what it would be like for them very soon.

As they counted down the weeks—only seven more until Milly's due date—AJ was spending more and more time with her. They'd become friends the way Milly had requested. Completely platonic. The only intimacy they shared was when he went to her doctor's appointments with her and that wasn't really intimate.

He spent every Saturday night at her place watching whatever movie she wanted to watch while he rubbed her feet and her swollen ankles. Not once had AJ felt as though he was forced into this, either. In fact, he'd been the one to insist he ease as much of her discomfort as he could.

And with every passing minute, AJ was falling more and more in love with the woman. He hadn't bothered to tell her that, not wanting to scare Milly off. He knew she would run the instant she thought he was in over his head. That had happened quite a while ago, but he wasn't going to share that, either.

So, rather than try to push things along, AJ was taking it one day at a time, enjoying every single moment, and secretly hoping that Milly was falling in love with him, too.

*

Tuesday, February 7

MILLY WAS ANTSY.

She wasn't sure if that was because AJ was so close and because he smelled so good or if there was something else at play. She enjoyed being with AJ, and she liked that he'd come over to help her babysit. Although babysit was probably a stretch for what she was doing. Considering Roan had put Liam to bed before he left, Milly was pretty much guarding the house and that was it.

"Wanna watch a movie?" AJ asked, glancing over at her.

She wondered if he could feel the tension, too. It was there every time they were together. Ever since she'd told him she was pregnant, they'd become friends.

Not more than friends.

Not friends with benefits even.

Just plain old boring friends.

Sometimes she wished for more.

That was probably her hormones talking, though.

"I don't care," she told him.

Before he could flip through the channels to find something to watch, there was a knock on the front door.

Milly's gaze slammed into AJ's. It was midnight, for goodness sake. Who in the world was showing up at Roan's house in the middle of the night?

"Probably Cam," AJ said, getting to his feet. "He jetted out of here so fast, probably forgot his key."

Milly nodded, watching AJ as he walked to the door.

Damn, the guy had a nice butt.

Like, really nice.

Again, hormones talking.

AJ frowned after peering through the security hole. "It's Roan's dad."

It took more than a little effort, but Milly managed to get to her feet. Being a million months pregnant was a pain in the butt.

"Want me to open it?" he whispered, his gaze imploring her.

"Yeah." Milly had a few things she wanted to say to this man. She'd heard all about the crap he was pulling with Roan, and she didn't much care for it.

AJ opened the door and Milly joined him, staring at the newcomers. Not only was Roan's dad standing on the porch but Roan's stepmonster—the nickname Milly had not-so-lovingly given the woman—was there, too.

"Roan's not here right now," Milly informed them. "Is everything all right?"

Daniel, Roan's father, looked a little put out to be standing there when he should've been sleeping, but Milly didn't miss the nudge Lydia gave him.

"We wanted to check on Liam," Daniel said with a sigh.

"He's asleep."

"Where's Roan?" Lydia questioned. "It's the middle of the night. He should be home with Liam."

"He ran an errand," Milly lied effortlessly. "He should be back any minute now."

"Then we'll wait," Lydia stated, pushing her way into the house.

No, Milly wasn't fond of this woman. She'd met her on the day of Cassie's funeral, and something about the woman had put her off then.

AJ placed his hand on her shoulder and gently guided Milly out of the way.

"I … uh…" Milly did not want to sit here with these people. "Why don't I tell Roan that you stopped by?"

Lydia's gaze dropped to Milly's left hand, then her belly, then up to AJ.

No way could Milly resist rolling her eyes.

"Lydia," Daniel said softly, his eyes searching the room. "I think she's right. We should go home."

"I need to know that Liam's safe in this house."

Okay, so maybe her hormones were a little out of whack from the pregnancy, but Milly did not miss the accusation in the woman's tone.

"Liam's perfectly safe," Milly told her.

"I'll check for myself."

"Uh, no." Milly was not going to let this woman come into Roan's house while he wasn't here. "He's asleep and I don't want him woken up."

Lydia paused, once again glancing down at Milly's belly.

"As a soon-to-be mother," Lydia began, "I would think you would understand my concern."

Milly lifted an eyebrow. "Actually, no. I don't."

"Is that man Roan's dating going to come back here with him?" Lydia inquired.

"Uh…" Milly glanced over at AJ, then back to Lydia. "I'm not sure. Not that it's any of your business. Or mine, for that matter."

"It is if you're at all worried about Liam."

Okay, enough was enough. Milly was tired and she wanted to sit down. Motioning toward the door, she forced a smile. "Well, I'm happy to say that Liam's perfectly fine. And he's more than safe with Roan and his boyfriend."

And yes, she added that part just to piss the woman off.

Lydia's gaze moved to Daniel, a line forming between her eyebrows.

"If you don't mind," Daniel said with a huff, "we'd like to take Liam back to our house tonight. We need to talk to Roan about a few things, and we can do that when he comes to pick him up."

Milly's back straightened and her anger exploded.

"No. First of all, I'm babysitting for Roan. He didn't mention you coming over at all, so I think it would be best that you leave." She turned her attention to Daniel. "If he chooses to come talk to you and he wants to bring Liam along, he can do that tomorrow."

"Young lady," Daniel snarled, his hand lifting as he pointed toward the back of the house, "that is my grandson in there and I have every right to—"

"Actually, you don't," Milly snapped. "Go. Now."

AJ's warm hand curled around her waist and Milly appreciated the comfort. She could tell he was on edge, but he was doing his best to stay out of it. With him there, she felt safe. Then again, with him there, she felt a lot of things.

Lydia started to the bedroom and Milly stepped directly in front of her.

"I don't think so."

"I will call the police if I need to," Lydia stated softly.

"Well, you need to," Milly countered. "Because I am damn sure not letting you leave this house with Liam. And if you try, I'll call the police myself. That's kidnapping."

The woman's eyes grew wide. She probably wasn't used to anyone standing up to her, but Milly wasn't a pushover. There were a million things she wanted to say to Lydia Gregory, and she'd managed to keep her mouth shut so far. She was playing nice.

That wasn't going to last much longer.

Nine

THEIR DAUGHTER IS BORN

THIS WASN'T AT all how AJ had expected to spend the evening.

The moment Roan's father and his father's wife showed up, he'd known the shit was going to hit the fan. AJ knew what was going on thanks to all the conversations taking place between Gannon and Milly these days. To make a long story short, everyone was worried about Roan. After his sister's death, he'd taken custody of Liam. During that time, he'd been fighting his father and stepmother because they didn't believe Roan could be a good parent because he was gay. Yep. They were stupid, but whatever.

Of course, Roan was dealing with a romantic entanglement, as well, but denying that. Hence the reason everyone was worried about him. And they had every right to be.

"I think it's best you leave," AJ insisted, feeling Milly's tension rise.

"We're not—"

"Oh, God," Milly groaned, clutching her big, round belly. "AJ. Ugh." She moaned loudly, holding her stomach.

AJ's gaze shot up to Daniel. "You take your wife and go right fucking now or I'll escort you both to the street."

Daniel looked almost apologetic when he nodded. His hand curled around Lydia's arm as he led her away. AJ shut the door and turned to Milly.

"Sit down," he ordered. "You need to relax."

"You're right," she said in a pained whisper. "That's what I need. Relax. I'll just sit on the couch and we can watch a movie."

He helped her to the sofa, keeping an eye on her every movement. Her forehead was creased and he suspected she wasn't telling him everything. Of course, his heart was beating a million miles a minute. While she wasn't due for a few more weeks…

"I'll get you a glass of water," he told her, not wanting her to see his concern.

"Thank you." She leaned back against the cushions.

AJ went to the kitchen and grabbed a glass. He didn't know his way around Roan's house the way he did Milly's but he figured it out quickly.

"AJ!" Milly screamed.

He dropped the glass into the sink with a loud clatter and raced into the living room. "What's wrong? Are you all right?"

Milly was breathing hard, clutching her belly as she leaned over. "I'm in labor."

Son of a bitch.

"Okay." He thrust his hand through his hair. "All right. Well. We need to get you to the hospital."

"You need to call Gannon."

"Yes. I do. Wait. Why?"

"Because Liam's here."

Shit. Liam was there. "Right. I'll call Gannon," he assured her. "And then I'll get Liam."

"And his car seat," Milly added.

"Yes, that, too."

While he headed for Liam's room, AJ reined in his panic and called Gannon. He had his phone number for exactly this reason. In case Milly went into labor when Gannon wasn't around.

"Hey, man," he said to Gannon when he answered. "We had a little snafu tonight." Okay, maybe he sounded a little too carefree. "Roan's dad and stepmonster—uh ... I mean stepmom showed up. They caused a scene. Milly got a little miffed, told them off. Then, of course, she went into labor." His voice rose on the end of the word, but he continued. "I'm grabbing Liam and his car seat, along with Milly, and we're heading for the hospital." AJ wasn't sure he breathed once during that.

"Yeah. Okay. Thanks for calling, AJ. We'll meet you at the hospital."

Hmm. Gannon sounded oddly calm right then. Had he been doing it for AJ? Maybe Gannon could feel AJ's panic? Or was he dealing with Roan? Maybe he was in the middle of something.

Shit. Milly was having the baby!

Thank God Gannon didn't ask a lot of questions. For one, AJ didn't have a lot of answers. Nor did he have a lot of time.

"Hey, buddy," he greeted Liam when he lifted the little boy from his crib. "We're gonna make a midnight trip. But don't worry, you can sleep in the car if you'd like."

AJ cradled the little boy to his chest and headed back out to the living room.

Milly was standing there, her hand on her belly and Liam's diaper bag over her shoulder. He quickly relieved her of that, then handed her the keys to lock Roan's house.

With the baby in his arms, the car seat dangling from his hand, and the diaper bag over his shoulder, AJ hurried to his truck. He tried to keep his cool but he was quickly losing his shit.

The doctor had already informed Milly she could deliver any day now. He said it wasn't unusual for a woman to have the baby a few weeks early, sometimes a few weeks late. He prayed that Miranda—yes, that was the name they'd already given her—was healthy and happy. Otherwise, AJ was going to track down Roan's father and beat him within an inch of his life.

Milly joined him at the truck a minute later. After placing Liam in his car seat and snapping everything into place, he pulled a small blanket from the diaper bag and laid it over him.

He once again composed himself when he shut the door and turned to Milly. He opened the front passenger door and helped her in before practically running around to the driver's side.

"I'm gonna need someone to get my bag from home," Milly said as they pulled out of Roan's neighborhood. "It's all ready to go."

"I know," he told her. She'd gone over the plan with him at least two dozen times. She already had a bag packed for her as well as another for Miranda.

"Plus, you'll have to make sure we get her car seat."

"There's plenty of time," he assured her.

Milly's breaths increased and her hands cradled her belly.

"Breathe," he instructed, trying to keep his voice calm although he felt anything but.

AJ had thought about what the birth of his child would be like at least million times, thought for sure it would be just like any old day.

He couldn't have been more wrong.

*

MILLY WAS SO glad she had opted for the epidural. She'd never in her life experienced anything as painful as the contractions that stole her breath and her sanity at the same time.

She thought for sure she was dying, despite the fact AJ assured her that wasn't the case. The entire time she'd been in labor, AJ had stood stoically by her side. He was her strength in the storm, and while she had yelled a few times, she knew she could never have done it without him there.

But it was over.

The labor had been intense, but there were no complications. Well, none with Miranda, anyway. There had been some touch-and-go moments with AJ. At one point, as soon as Milly had started to push, she thought he was going to pass out. Thankfully for everyone involved, that hadn't happened.

And now he was over with the nurse as they prepared Miranda to come to her. Every few seconds, he would look over at her and smile. Her heart swelled as she watched him. He was a godsend, her rock.

And now they had a daughter.

Miranda Lynn Ballard.

She and AJ had picked out the name together, spending hours tossing around various options, many of which they had laughed about, quite a few they had vetoed. But Miranda was the perfect name for the perfect baby.

Eight pounds, six ounces with a head full of dark hair. She was the most beautiful thing Milly had ever seen, and so far, she'd only gotten a brief glimpse of her.

The instant Milly heard her baby's first cry, her heart had swelled to the size of the earth. Not only for Miranda but also for AJ. Having him there with her… She couldn't imagine having to have done this alone.

Granted, AJ was still taking the friends thing very seriously. Of course, she wasn't putting much effort into seducing him or anything. Not when being friends was her idea. Why was it her idea again?

Of course, it had helped that she'd been as big as a house. It was hard to want to seduce the sexiest man alive when she felt like a blimp most days. Not that she hadn't enjoyed the pregnancy, but sometimes, when her skin felt two sizes too small for her expanding belly, the thought of showing any part of herself had been frightening.

As AJ approached, a huge smile on his face, Milly felt her heart melt a little. She loved this man. Even if she would never tell him. She was so grateful he was Miranda's father. And he would be an amazing father. That much was a given. He had a heart of gold.

The nurse appeared with Miranda wrapped in a little pink blanket. As the woman rested the tiny little bundle on her chest, Milly's heart turned over.

This was quite possibly the best day of her life. She honestly hadn't expected to ever be a mother. Not because she didn't want kids. She'd always wanted them, but she'd never seen herself in a relationship strong enough to bring one into the world. While she and AJ weren't technically together, Milly knew they would be great parents together.

As for anything more than that…

Well, Milly hoped that one day things would work out the way they were supposed to. She wasn't going to get her hopes up, because that never worked out for her. However, she was going to keep going the way they'd been for the past few months. And maybe, if things were meant to be, then something would come of it.

If not, at least she had AJ in her life.

That was more than she'd ever anticipated in the first place.

Ten

IT'S BEEN SO LONG

Twelve weeks later, May 2

AJ CARRIED MIRANDA into her bedroom, setting her sleeping form in her crib. The room was decked out in pink and white, the perfect setting for his little princess. While Miranda had a room at his house, she'd never stayed there. Instead, AJ had made a habit of spending nights in Milly's guest room so he didn't disrupt Miranda's routine.

Well, not only for that reason. He stayed at Milly's because he wanted to be there with Miranda. He didn't want to miss anything, plus it had given him the opportunity to take care of Milly. He knew Milly would've allowed him to take Miranda to his place if he wanted. However, he saw no reason to when he could spend time with both of his girls this way.

Not that Milly belonged to him. She still kept him in the friend zone, and honestly, it was driving him mad. But he had learned to cope. Their awkwardly designed little family was working out great and the last thing AJ wanted to do was to cause any disruption to that.

"Good night, princess," he whispered to his daughter as he stared down at her. She was the most precious thing in the world. Over the past three months, he'd learned as much as he could on how to take care of her and he was doing a rather good job, if he did say so himself.

The thought made him smile as he reached down and touched her tiny hand. God, he loved her. Far more than he'd ever thought possible.

"Sleep tight," he said as he backed away from her crib. She would be up in roughly three hours for her late-night feeding, and until then, he would get some quality time with Milly.

He closed the door as quietly as he could and headed back to the living room. Milly was curled up in the corner of the couch, her eyes tracking him when he approached.

"So what are we gonna watch tonight?" she asked when he settled in beside her.

They weren't close enough to touch, but he knew Milly liked to curl up against him when they were watching movies and he definitely didn't mind, so he ensured she knew she was welcome.

"I get to pick?" he teased. "Because that's never happened before."

Milly giggled. "Is there something specific you wanna watch?"

"Not necessarily." He honestly didn't care. As long as Milly was happy, he could watch anything.

And he had. For months, he'd spent many of his Friday and Saturday nights watching a variety of movies. Most of them chick flicks. Milly had a fondness for Nicholas Sparks and he was sure they'd seen them all at this point. He figured that was the direction she would go tonight, and it truly didn't make a difference to him.

"I was thinking we could watch Fifty Shades of Grey."

AJ knew his eyes were likely bugging out of his head. He had no earthly idea what the movie entailed, but from the previews he'd seen forever ago, it looked as though it was mostly about sex.

Milly giggled. "Or will that offend your prudish sensibilities?"

His eyes narrowed. "Did you just call me a prude?"

A full laugh escaped Milly as he inched closer.

AJ knew this was dangerous territory, but he couldn't help himself. It had been far too long since he'd had his hands on this woman and he was desperate for her. The cruise had taken place on May thirtieth of last year and since they were back around to May again, the one-year mark was quickly approaching. He wanted nothing more than to have her beneath him, her luscious body surrounded by him while he consumed her in every way imaginable.

Milly giggled, then aimed the remote at the television. "Fifty Shades it is."

Knowing he had to take a step back before he did something to ruin what they'd spent months building, AJ tickled her, then inched back to his spot.

A few minutes later, the movie started.

For a solid hour, he watched Milly watching the movie. AJ couldn't find any interest in what was on the screen. Well, aside from the random moaning he heard. That was rather appealing. Too much, in fact.

Milly had moved closer as the minutes ticked by until she was practically lying with her head on his thigh, her attention on the screen. In a completely platonic way, AJ had rested his arm on her shoulder, and over time, it had drifted down to her side, behind her arm. Only, Milly had started shifting onto her back, which meant his hand was now pressed against the side of her breast.

He wasn't sure she was aware of what she was doing, but he was. His dick damn sure was. If she was completely innocent in this, then he was a dog. Otherwise, this woman was playing with fire and there was no way this night ended like the last year's worth of nights.

Figuring he would play the game—if there was a game—AJ remained where he was, ignoring the throbbing behind his zipper as he gently brushed his thumb against the side of her breast every so often.

"AJ?" Milly's gaze shot to him.

"Hmm?" He pretended to be watching the television before glancing down at her.

Her breathing had increased, her chest rising and falling, matching the pounding of his heart. This was the moment of truth. If she wasn't playing with him, he knew she would make a move. Milly wasn't shy.

When her hand came over and wrapped around his wrist, he knew it could go one of two ways. Either she would move his hand off her and things would get rather awkward, or she would move his hand so that it covered her breast and then all bets were off at that point.

He held his breath, waiting to see what she would do.

AJ's dick jerked in his jeans when she tugged his hand so that it covered her breast. He couldn't contain the growl that erupted in his chest.

"Milly…" He didn't mean it to come out as a warning, but that was exactly how it sounded.

"Please, AJ." She pressed her hand over his, forcing him to cup her breast.

He knew this was not a good idea. All this time they'd maintained a perfectly good friendship and now they were going to cross a line they probably couldn't go back from.

But he wasn't a fucking saint.

His body took over, his thumb brushing over her nipple. She turned her attention back to the television while he fondled her gently. He wasn't going to rush this, and he prayed like hell she didn't change her mind.

Her soft moans said she was enjoying what he was doing to her. After a few minutes, he got bolder, sliding his hand beneath her T-shirt and tugging her bra cup down until his palm grazed the soft, smooth flesh.

Milly's back bowed as she arched into him and AJ knew that this was not going to end in a platonic fashion.

Not by a long shot.

*

MILLY WAS GOING to go out of her mind. Her skin was too tight, her body primed and eager for whatever AJ wanted to do to her. She'd waited so long for him to touch her again, silently willing him to simply take matters into his own hands.

Since he hadn't done that, Milly had taken the lead. Tonight, she'd decided to be the instigator. Part of her had feared AJ would reject her, but based on his rapid breaths, that wasn't the direction he was going.

She wanted to blame this on her hormones. Ever since she had Miranda, she'd been on fire. She wanted AJ with a passion that rivaled all, even if it wasn't the best idea she'd ever had.

Right now, it was the only idea.

Arching into his hand, Milly moaned softly. She tried to focus on the television, enjoying the impromptu make-out session. However, that became impossible when he raised her T-shirt and freed her breast. The cool air kissed her skin, making her hotter than before.

Minutes passed while he teased and tormented her nipple. Milly was barely hanging on when AJ cleared his throat.

"Take off the shirt," he instructed. "And the bra."

Without a second thought, Milly sat up enough to discard the items he'd mentioned before tossing them onto the coffee table. She lay back down, her head once again resting on his rock-hard thigh. His hand resumed the mind-boggling torment, although this time, he teased both breasts, pinching her nipples until she was sighing and moaning in earnest.

Milly squeezed her thighs together, trying to ease the ache that had ignited. She was so wet, so ready for him.

"Unbutton your shorts," he insisted.

Milly quickly worked the button free and lowered the zipper.

AJ's hand traveled down her stomach, his fingers dipping into her shorts, then beneath the elastic band of her panties. She held her breath, desperate for him to touch her, to bring her to orgasm, to alleviate this god-awful ache.

But AJ's fingers stopped just short of where she wanted him.

"Tell me," AJ growled. "Tell me what you want, Milly."

"You to touch me," she replied, the words said on a breathless moan.

"Where?"

"My pussy." His fingers slid a little lower. "Please. Touch my clit. I hurt so bad."

Another growl escaped him as his thick finger pressed against the swollen bundle of nerves. Within seconds, she was writhing against him, chasing that damn release that would offer some relief.

Milly moaned, saying his name over and over as he worked her to the brink only to back off at the last second. When she couldn't take any more, Milly shoved her shorts and panties down her thighs, then managed to kick them off. She lay there completely naked, not caring that her body wasn't quite the same as before she'd had Miranda. She had stretch marks on her belly and the sides of her breasts, but they didn't bother her. This was her new reality and she embraced it wholeheartedly.

AJ's wicked fingers continued teasing, rubbing her clit to the point of insanity. She was bracing herself for his retreat, only he didn't. This time, AJ continued to rub until the electricity sparked in her core, her orgasm igniting. She gritted her teeth and came in a hard, blinding rush. Every nerve in her body felt the tidal wave of pleasure that slammed into her.

It took a few minutes for her to come down from that long-awaited high, but when she did, Milly sat up and turned to face AJ.

She met his gaze and held it. "I want to suck you."

He groaned, as though that was the best and worst idea he'd ever heard. Maybe they could keep this simple. Without blurring the lines with intercourse. If she got him off with her mouth, perhaps they could put this behind them, go back to where they'd been an hour ago.

Friends.

AJ didn't make a move to unbutton his jeans and Milly started to feel self-conscious. What if he didn't find her attractive now that she was hanging out in all her post-baby glory? She'd almost lost the weight she'd gained, but she still had about five pounds to go. What if he didn't like it? What if she didn't turn him on the way she had before?

With his eyes still focused on the television, AJ finally gave in to her request. He began unbuttoning his jeans, lowering the zipper. His head fell back when he freed his cock. Milly watched, completely enraptured as he began stroking himself slowly.

Her eyes locked on the silver piercing, and her mouth watered. That blasted piercing was what had gotten them to this point. Well, her fascination with it, anyway. There was no denying that Milly had thought about his pierced cock for months, ever since she'd seen it the first time.

"Put your mouth on me, beautiful. Let me feel those lips around my dick."

His words sent a shockwave through her system, and she didn't hesitate, leaning over and teasing the swollen head with her tongue. She fondled the ring with her tongue, loving the way he hissed when she did. AJ's hand rested on her back, sliding down her spine as she knelt beside him.

Milly went to work pleasing him, doing all the things she knew he enjoyed. Using her tongue, she worked his shaft, licking, sucking. She cupped his balls, feeling the way they began drawing up closer to his body. He was on edge, the same way she had been before he'd given her a reprieve.

"Suck me, beautiful. Fuck, Milly. Suck me."

She did, taking him as deep as she could while his hand trailed over her ass, his fingers probing between her legs. When he slid one finger into her, Milly moaned. The vibration must've triggered something in AJ, because his other hand twined in her hair as he held her in place. His hips began thrusting upward, filling her mouth, while his imploring fingers began fucking her.

There was no way she was going to last. Not with him fingering her so perfectly. Milly didn't want to come without him, though. She focused all her attention on bringing him to orgasm, moaning softly, ensuring he knew just how much she needed him like this.

"Mill … fuck … I'm gonna come in your mouth. Suck me. Harder. I need to come."

She hollowed out her cheeks, sucking fiercely, desperate to send him over even as a second release built in her core. His fingers worked the nerve endings that had been dormant for so long. It was impossible to ignore.

As her insides coiled, her body burning hotter, brighter, Milly focused on him.

When AJ groaned, his fingers tightening in her hair, she felt the first pulse of his cock, the warning that he was about to fill her mouth. She didn't release him, sucking firmly, ready to drink him down.

His fingers pounded into her. Milly's muscles clamped around those glorious digits as her orgasm ripped through her. When she moaned this time, it was loud and vulgar.

"Fuck, yes," AJ hissed. "I'm coming, beautiful. Take all of me."

And just like that, they crossed a line Milly knew they shouldn't be crossing. Despite her need, her deep-seated love for this man, Milly wasn't willing to risk losing him. She obviously wasn't cut out for a relationship, her past proving that.

But what did she do now?

It wasn't like she could apologize.

Could she?

Eleven

CAN'T GET ENOUGH

Four days later

AJ HADN'T BEEN back to Milly's since Saturday morning, when he'd slipped out after giving Miranda her morning bottle while Milly slept in.

That Friday night had leveled him. Their make-out session on the couch, Milly sucking him off, him making her come with his fingers had left AJ wanting more.

Granted, Milly had retreated almost instantly. She'd acted as though nothing had happened. When she finally excused herself for bed, AJ had sat on her couch for the longest time, trying to figure out what the hell had happened. They'd been moving in the right direction.

Or so he'd thought.

Apparently, Milly wasn't on the same wavelength.

So, AJ had done the only thing he knew to do. He had retreated as well. While he texted Milly constantly to see how she and Miranda were doing, he had opted to stay away. Of course, his texts included as many requests for pictures as he could get. Every couple of hours, Milly was sending pictures. Some of Miranda—awake, asleep, smiling, sitting in her swing—and some of Milly, both with and without Miranda. He loved those damn pictures. In fact, he had saved every single one to his phone so he could look at them whenever he wanted.

Being away from them was painful. Four days felt like an eternity. When Milly texted him a short time ago and asked him to come over for dinner, AJ had wanted to tell her no. He wanted to see if pushing her would bring Milly closer.

Only he couldn't do that.

AJ missed his girls too much to stay away. So now, as he climbed out of his truck in front of her house, he steeled himself for tonight. He intended to go inside, have dinner, spend a couple of hours with Miranda before going home for the night. That was the smart thing to do.

No movies, no make-out sessions, no sleeping in the guest room.

He was going to hold his ground and hope Milly came around.

Damn near every one of his good intentions went right out the window when Milly answered the door wearing that pretty little sundress, her hair pulled up, showing off the delicate lines of her neck.

This woman was going to be the death of him.

"Hey," she greeted with a smile. "You're right on time."

It was obvious she was pretending the other night hadn't happened, so he would, too.

"Right on time? For?"

He stepped into the house and closed the door behind him.

"Miranda just went to sleep and dinner's almost ready. The only thing left is to finish making the salad."

"What can I do to help?"

"Pour the tea?"

"With pleasure."

AJ followed Milly into the kitchen. There was tension between them. He could feel it. Something potent and powerful. It wrapped around his chest and squeezed. His cock thickened just from the memory of the other night. Not to mention, seeing Milly's beautiful legs beneath that damn dress.

He wondered if she was wearing panties. It wouldn't be difficult to figure out.

Not that he would.

Nope. He wasn't giving in. Milly clearly wanted friendship and he would give her that. They could chalk the other night up to their libidos. Neither of them had had sex in almost a year. It was only natural for something like that to happen between two consenting adults.

Christ. As he filled two glasses with ice, he remembered how warm and wet her pussy had been. How Milly had moaned and sighed, urging him to make her come.

His dick was already hard, but he ignored the incessant throbbing as he headed back over to the counter where the tea pitcher was sitting. AJ had to lean around Milly to reach it, his body far too close to hers. So close he was touching her.

When his cock pressed against her ass, she inhaled sharply, a soft moan escaping her.

Fucking hell.

AJ stood there. Unable to move, unable to think. His body took charge, his cock gently rubbing against her ass while he cupped her hip in his hand.

"AJ..."

Yeah. The way she said his name wasn't helping. Breathless and eager. She wanted this as much as he did.

He forgot about the tea, the glasses, dinner. Nothing mattered but the warmth of her skin, the sweet scent of her that went right to his head.

AJ leaned down and nuzzled her neck.

"You're killing me, woman," he whispered, gently squeezing her hip.

Milly leaned into him, her ass grinding against his dick.

This was stupid. If he didn't move away, he knew what was coming next. He would grab a condom from his wallet, sheath himself, and within seconds, he could be buried inside her. Heaven awaited him in the form of her tight, wet pussy.

Milly stopped what she was doing, and for the life of him, AJ couldn't even remember what that was.

Salad. Right. She was making salad so they could have dinner. He was supposed to come over, have dinner, spend time with Miranda, then go home and sleep in his own fucking bed. Alone.

Milly leaned into him, her back pressing against his chest as her hand covered his. She guided it from her hip to her pussy as she tugged her dress up.

"Please, AJ."

"Please what?" he urged.

"Fuck me."

He groaned, a tormented sound. She was killing him.

AJ wanted to be a gentleman. He wanted to refuse her because he knew this was going nowhere. Despite the fact that he wanted more from her, Milly wasn't giving him the same impression. The other night, she'd slipped away as soon as they both came. Gone was the feisty, sexy woman whose lips were so fucking perfect he jacked off to the thought of them damn near every night. In her place, the friend he'd come to know so well.

AJ didn't want to be friends with Milly. Well, he didn't want to be only friends with her. He wanted this woman to sleep beside him every night, to wake up in his arms.

Unfortunately, he knew she didn't want the same thing.

But this ... this unbridled passion. It was impossible to ignore. He was still just a man. And she was the only woman he wanted.

"AJ. Please."

"Right here," he said. "Beg me one more time, Milly, and I'm going to lift up this dress and fuck you right here in your kitchen. I'm going to bury my cock inside you, feel your wet pussy squeeze me."

He groaned, his own words making his dick throb painfully.

"Yes." As though to emphasize her acquiescence, Milly pressed her ass against him as she leaned forward, her hands landing on the counter.

AJ couldn't resist. She was driving him absolutely insane. He grabbed his wallet, pulled out the lone condom he'd tucked in there, and within a minute, he had his cock in his hand, sheathed and eager.

"Bend over," he insisted.

When she did, AJ shoved her dress up to her hips. The silky white panties she had on pulled another rough groan from him. He shoved them down her hips, allowing them to slide down her legs to the floor. Milly stepped out of them, and before she was firmly on two feet again, AJ was guiding his cock into her from behind.

He went as slow as his body would allow. Milly bent at the waist, her hands gripping the countertop. She moaned.

"Yes," she whimpered. "Please fuck me, AJ."

Knowing this wasn't going to end the way he wanted, AJ gave in to his dark urges. He would deal with the fallout later.

Right now, the only thing he cared about was the warm, wet clasp of her pussy.

*

MILLY HAD PROMISED herself she wouldn't allow this to happen tonight.

She had felt incredibly guilty since Friday night, when she had gone to her bedroom alone after they'd brought each other to orgasm in her living room.

However, Milly wanted AJ with a passion so powerful it threatened to take her out at the knees. Despite the fact that she knew this would never work out, she was selfish. Her body craved his.

She wanted to give herself over to him completely. Not just physically but emotionally as well. Except she wasn't capable of that. She'd spent too long believing she wasn't worthy, that she couldn't make anyone happy. Which meant, once this was over, she would retreat again and then she would have to deal with the disappointment on AJ's face.

He pressed his hips forward, his cock tunneling into her. Her body gripped him tightly, painfully. It had been so long, yet it felt like just yesterday since they'd last done this. Since Milly had welcomed AJ into her body.

"Fuck, yes," he hissed. "You're so tight."

She loved his dirty talk, the way he said what was on his mind. He was the take-control kind of guy and that did it for her in so many ways.

"I can't be easy, Milly," he warned, his palm landing between her shoulder blades as he pushed her down toward the countertop. "Hold on, beautiful."

She did. And AJ didn't disappoint. He fucked her right there in her kitchen, her dress hiked up to her waist, her panties on the floor at her feet. It was so erotic, just thinking about how they looked had her careening toward an orgasm that would likely blow her mind.

AJ held on to her hips, driving into her. She moaned with every punishing thrust, her pussy filled, stretched. It was exquisite. Milly hadn't expected to ever have AJ like this again. Now she wasn't sure she wanted to go back to that friendship.

"God, yes," he growled.

Milly whimpered as he impaled her, his rough grip making her bite her lip. She let him ride her from behind, to use her for his own pleasure while she took hers in return. He lit her up from the inside out, the tension coiling tightly as she inched toward release. She didn't want to come. Not yet. Milly wanted to ride the wave for as long as possible.

As though he knew what she wanted, AJ took his time, fucking her endlessly. Her voice became rough the more she moaned and screamed, loving every second of having him inside her.

When he leaned over her, his hips jerking in short, rapid strokes, Milly groaned. His hand left her hip, sliding between her thighs until his fingers were rubbing her clit.

"I want you to come all over my cock," he whispered. "Then I'm gonna fuck you some more, Milly. I'm gonna make you come again and again."

Yes! She wanted that so much.

Milly allowed him to send her higher and higher with his cock and his fingers until she felt as though she was floating outside her body. When her orgasm detonated, it stole her voice and her mind at the same time.

"Just like that, beautiful. Oh, fuck … come all over my cock."

AJ didn't stop. He continued to drive into her again and again until another orgasm was building, this one as powerful as the first. His fingers worked her clit until she was teetering on the razor-sharp edge once more.

When her climax struck her, Milly screamed, her pussy clamping down on him.

AJ groaned, slamming into her once, twice.

"I'm coming," he growled roughly. "Fuck. I'm coming."

Milly spent a few minutes trying to catch her breath, AJ's warm body still pressed against her. When he finally pulled out, she stood up, straightening her dress while AJ disappeared toward the bathroom.

A few minutes later, he returned. His eyes didn't meet hers and Milly felt a sense of loss. He was the one retreating.

Milly knew she had to talk to him. They had to discuss what had happened between them and how they would handle this going forward. Could they make something work? Did he want that?

Before he made it to the kitchen, a soft whimper sounded from the baby monitor on the counter. A few seconds later, Miranda let out her familiar cry, a signal that she was wet or hungry or both.

AJ peered up at her as he stopped. "I'll get her."

Nodding, Milly tried to pretend she was back to working on the salad.

Whatever had just happened, Milly knew this wasn't going to end well. They had effectively crossed that line.

Now the question was whether they moved forward or back. And who was going to make that decision.

Twelve

HINT. HINT.

Two weeks later

"THESE INSTRUCTIONS ARE ridiculous," Milly grumbled as she stared down at the unfolded paper in front of her.

AJ sat in Milly's living room watching as she sat cross-legged on the floor, staring at the instructions for the new baby toy she'd insisted Miranda needed. Something that was supposed to entertain their almost four-month-old daughter with flashing lights and holes for oversized blocks to be put in.

"Want some help?"

Milly smiled up at him. "What? No faith?"

AJ chuckled. "I've got all the faith in the world."

For the past two weeks, ever since the incident in the kitchen, AJ had gone back to his routine of coming over to

Milly's damn near every day in an effort to spend time with Milly and their daughter.

However, AJ couldn't erase that day from his mind. He thought about it endlessly. Yet he had somehow managed to keep his distance, even when he was at her house. It wasn't easy, but he knew it was necessary. He had to be careful when dealing with Milly. The last thing he wanted was to scare her off.

In an effort to keep their friendship in the forefront, the Friday and Saturday night movie marathons were a thing of the past. AJ had come to that decision, and Milly had respected that. He knew he couldn't keep his hands off her if he was that close, so he figured it was better this way.

The first couple of days after, Milly had been tense. Then again, so had he. AJ wasn't sure what to make of their encounter, and although he wanted more, he was trying to give Milly some space. He was grateful that Milly had relaxed a bit since then, allowing them to ease back into their close friendship.

Unfortunately, it didn't seem to matter how many hints he dropped, Milly wasn't picking up on the fact that AJ was doing his best to convince her to take a chance on him. A real chance. As in the three of them becoming an official family. They were technically a family already, but he wanted a ring on Milly's finger and a place in her bed.

Yes, they had a kid together. Yes, they'd had some seriously amazing sex a few times, starting a lifetime ago when he'd first met her. And yes, from the moment Milly had informed him she'd gotten pregnant from their naked adventures, he'd done the right thing and stood beside her every step of the way.

He tried to tell himself things were better this way, but he knew that was bullshit. He respected Milly and he was doing his damnedest to pretend those last two encounters hadn't happened, but he couldn't. Every night when he went to bed alone, he missed her.

He'd hoped by giving her time, Milly would accept that they were meant to be.

Regrettably, she hadn't.

AJ was eager and ready for the next step in his relationship with Milly. Granted, he didn't know what that next step was. They'd become partners in this parenting thing, but he wanted so much more than that. However, every time he thought about striking up a conversation with her about it, Milly would come up with some crazy idea and he'd be forced to put it on the back burner. It was as though she could read his mind and the topic wasn't on her list of things to tackle.

"Seriously," Milly muttered. "How does anyone ever get these things put together?" Her light blue eyes lifted to his face. "I'm sure I'm making it more complicated than it is."

AJ grinned. "I'm sure you are, too."

"Hey." She pretended to be offended, but her smile was brilliant. "Let's see you give it a whirl."

Pushing to his feet, AJ closed the distance between them and took a seat on the floor beside Milly. He was careful not to touch her. It seemed whenever he did, she would blush and find a way to disappear from the room. He hadn't been able to pinpoint her responses, but he got the feeling she was as nervous as he was.

Which meant he simply needed to suck it up and make a move. To open the lines of communication by discussing what had happened and what they both wanted. Perhaps she would be open to something more from him.

And AJ wasn't just referring to a sexual relationship, although he was definitely hoping for that.

"Here," he said softly, keeping a smile on his face. "Let me look."

Before he could take the paper, Milly pulled it out of reach and spun around to face away from him.

"I changed my mind," she said with a giggle. "The last thing I need is for you to figure it out in a minute and make me look more clueless than I already am."

AJ couldn't help but smile. The woman always claimed she was clueless when it came to this parenting thing, but Milly had settled into it like she'd been born with the maternal gene. Sometimes she made him feel as though he was all thumbs, unsure what to do next.

Some people didn't know how to take Milly. She was overbearing, but deep down, it was only because she cared deeply for her friends and family. She had played a part in hooking up several of her friends, including nudging her best friend, Gannon, toward Cam almost two years ago. Milly had also stepped in and helped to rekindle the love Noah and Dare had from long ago.

And yes, there was something about Milly that drove him absolutely batshit crazy. It might've been her crooked smile, or the way she laughed so hard she cried. Perhaps it was her instigating nature, always ensuring she was sticking her nose where it didn't belong.

But most of all, AJ admired her heart. She loved fiercely. He only wished she could open herself up a little and allow him to love her.

Unfortunately, Milly wasn't having any of it. AJ didn't think she was playing hard to get, he believed she was merely hesitant when it came to her own relationships. She allowed him to get close but not too close.

He was ready to close the gap, to move this thing to the next level. He was eager to feel her beneath him once more, to have his lips caressing every silky inch of her. His dick was constantly hard, his need for her growing with every minute he spent with her.

When he met her, AJ had thought she was breathtaking. She'd gone from sexy to luscious during her pregnancy, driving him wild without even knowing it. And now, after having Miranda, she was even more striking than before.

For whatever reason, he got the feeling Milly didn't notice how head-over-heels in fucking love with her he truly was.

However, at some point, he knew he was going to have to tell her.

*

HE WAS TOO close.

Close enough Milly inhaled his familiar scent with every raspy breath she took. And the closer he got, the more she ached for him. Every time he stopped by the house, she told herself she would confront this thing between them, see if he was willing to explore something more than the co-parenting roles they'd assumed.

If only it were that easy. If only Milly hadn't pushed him away for so long, fearful that she would fall for the man only to have him move on to greener pastures. For most of her adult life, Milly had shrugged off the men who had come and gone from her life. However, she had always expected it, and never allowed herself to hope for something more.

Until AJ. Until she'd spent several days and nights with him, getting to know the man intimately. During the cruise, she had found herself completely transfixed with him. And she knew he had good intentions where she was concerned. After all, he had been by her side since the day she told him she was pregnant. She knew he wasn't one of those fly-by-night guys. And still she had a hard time convincing her heart that this was the risk she had to take or she would never truly be happy.

"Come on," he said, his deep voice making the hairs on her arms stand on end. "Let me help."

She missed his touch, the way he so easily brought her to a heightened state of awareness. Since the night in her kitchen, AJ hadn't touched her. Hell, he hardly looked at her sometimes and she knew it was all her fault. She had provoked him, overstepped their boundaries, and now she had to pay the price.

"Nope. I got it." She pretended to shield the paper from his view, silently pleading for him to move closer.

His long arms came around her, but he didn't touch. Not quite. "You've had your turn."

With every passing second, Milly fell for him a little more, and when he was with her, she'd never felt more alive.

Granted, there had been some bumps in the road on their path to get to this point and she wasn't innocent in any of it. In fact, it was her fault they hadn't explored their relationship potential a long time ago.

Yet he was still here, being the friend she'd always wanted. And he was an amazing dad. Miranda loved him to pieces and Milly really couldn't blame her. While her daughter was surrounded by wonderful men, Miranda's face didn't light up with any of them the way it did when AJ walked into a room.

From the moment she'd informed him he was going to be a father, AJ had embraced it. He had promised to stand beside her and he'd actually followed through. Even now, as he sat only a few feet away in her living room, giving in to her puny excuse that she needed help to put this toy together. It was a lie. She had already figured it out, but Milly had needed a reason to get him closer. She wanted the distance between them erased. It was time for something more.

And she was ready.

Mostly.

It didn't matter that he stopped by all the time and called even more. Milly texted him anytime Miranda did something that he didn't get to witness firsthand. She overwhelmed him with pictures and videos, not wanting him to miss out. But AJ was now keeping his distance from her while ensuring he remained close to his daughter.

It killed her. Every night when she crawled into bed after putting Miranda to sleep, Milly thought about AJ. She relived those moments from the cruise, from their heated movie night, the phenomenal sex in her kitchen. She was now fantasizing about what it would be like to have him there with them, sleeping in her bed, holding her through the night.

AJ didn't seem to be catching on, though. She constantly wondered why he wouldn't come closer when they were alone. Why wouldn't he give in and kiss her already? They hadn't kissed since the cruise. Not even that day in her kitchen. It wasn't like she hadn't given him a million clues over the past couple of weeks.

She feared she had pushed him too far.

"Hand it over," he said firmly, as though he knew she was teasing him.

Milly hunched over a little more, her insides warming from his nearness. "Not yet."

When his arms finally banded around her, she inhaled roughly, her skin prickling with awareness. She could've sworn she heard him hiss, as though touching her was more than he could stand.

"Milly." His voice had dropped a couple of octaves. "Give it up."

Was he referring to the instructions or the weird game they'd been playing?

"Not yet." She tried to laugh, but it came out breathless as she felt the heat of his body against her back.

Please. Just a little more.

"Milly…"

She could hear the strain in his voice. The warning the word implied sent a shiver down her spine. Did she dare test the waters? See if he was willing to simply give in? To let this thing between them ignite one more time? Could they confront it like adults this time around?

When his hand shifted to brush her hair back from her shoulder, Milly held her breath. He was touching her. Just a light graze of his finger, but it was more than she'd gotten from him in fourteen painfully long days.

Milly heard him inhale, felt the warmth of his breath on her neck. Her nipples instantly pebbled as the ache between her legs throbbed with every heartbeat. She wanted him more than she wanted air.

Just when she thought he would finally make his move, a startled cry sounded from the baby monitor on the table. Miranda's routine was like clockwork. Every night, about nine thirty, she would wake up, wanting to be changed and fed once more before she would sleep soundly until the sun came up.

Suddenly AJ moved away. "I'll get her," he said softly.

Unable to look at him, for fear he'd see all the desire she'd hidden from him for so long, Milly simply nodded. "I'll get her bottle ready."

And just like that, the moment was lost.

Thirteen

PULLING THE PUNCHES

Three days later, Friday

"YOU READY TO hit the gym?" AJ asked Hudson when he arrived at his brother's apartment above the marina shortly after three.

Charger, Teague's emotional support dog, was there to greet AJ with his attentive brown eyes.

"Hey, there, buddy," AJ greeted. "What's shakin'?" He squatted down to pet the dog.

Although Hudson was happily married, he still found time to hang out with AJ a few times a week, mostly when they went to the gym. Sometimes for dinner or an afternoon fishing. Now that AJ was in town more, they were able to get together a few times a week and AJ found he looked forward to it.

Give me five minutes, Hudson signed back.

"Sure thing. Where's Teague?"

Out on the water.

Because of the nice weather these past few weeks, Teague seemed to always be out on the water with clients. The marina was doing a lot of business, more so in recent years, in fact. While Teague worked mostly as a boat mechanic alongside Hudson, he did spend his fair share of time taking clients out when Cam, Dare, and Roan were otherwise busy. Most of the time they were out on the water as well.

A tap on his shoulder signaled Hudson's return. AJ shook out his shoulders, trying to let go of some of the stress he was carrying around lately. While almost everything in his life was going by the book—he had a stable job, a beautiful, healthy daughter, friends and family to hang with—there was still one aspect that was weighing heavily on his mind. It had everything to do with Milly and their inability to connect.

After you, Hudson signed, then motioned for the door.

He was walking down the stairs to the parking lot when Hudson tapped him again. AJ glanced over to see his brother signing.

What's your problem?

AJ laughed. "No problem. Just need to work off some of this restless energy."

Hudson headed for his truck and AJ followed. He was used to his brother wanting to drive. And truth was, AJ spent so much time traveling, he'd gotten used to sitting back and waiting to arrive somewhere. It no longer bothered him.

"Teague doing well?" AJ asked in an effort to make conversation.

Hudson replied with, He is.

"Good. Happy to hear it."

AJ was genuinely happy for Hudson. He'd found the love of his life and settled down. Although Hudson had fought his desires for Teague, he had finally given in despite what Hudson perceived as an age difference issue. Teague was almost ten years younger than Hudson. Not that it slowed either of them down at all.

While the couple had gone through some seriously rocky patches, AJ was glad to see Teague was no longer suffering in silence with his depression. Now that his friends were aware of his issues, they had become his rock-solid support system. It certainly made a huge difference.

They were halfway to the gym when AJ's cell phone chimed. He pulled it from his pocket and hit the button to see the message. It was from Milly and instantly his heart rate sped up.

He could feel Hudson's eyes on him as he opened up his text app and glanced at the message.

Would you mind watching Miranda tomorrow night?

AJ shot a quick text back. Of course not.

He took every opportunity to spend time with Miranda. Although he was still traveling for work, he was in the process of working out a deal to take over some of the local accounts so he could stick close to home. Miranda was growing up so quickly, and every second he was away, he felt as though he was missing out.

At first, his boss hadn't been too happy with AJ's suggestion, but when AJ told him it was either that or he would be seeking employment elsewhere, his boss had given in. Sometimes it paid to be good at your job.

His phone chimed with Milly's response: Thanks.

AJ's curiosity got the best of him and he messaged her again. Mind if I ask where you're going?

It wasn't like Milly to go out. And when she did, it was usually for dinner with Gannon so the two of them could catch up. Since AJ was usually out of town during those interactions, Cam was always in place to watch Miranda.

AJ stared at his phone, waiting for her response. When it came in, something cracked inside his chest.

Date.

"What the fuck?" AJ glared at the phone as though that would change the letters in that one fucking word. "What the hell does she mean she's got a date?"

Hudson smacked his arm, and AJ turned his attention to his brother. He could read the unspoken question on his face: What's wrong?

AJ shrugged. "Milly said she has a date tomorrow night. Wants to know if I'll watch Miranda."

Hudson's curiosity disappeared, replaced with something else.

How the hell could this be happening? Why would Milly be going out on a date? After what had happened between them? Maybe it'd only happened twice, but still. Didn't she realize he wanted something more from her? More than what they had going now?

126

AJ wanted to punch something. Namely one of the heavy bags at the gym. Maybe if he beat the shit out of it for a while he would feel better.

Then again, probably not.

After dropping his phone on his leg, AJ thrust his hand in his hair, jerking roughly. This couldn't be happening. What the fuck was he going to do if Milly ended up dating someone? Hell, what if she ended up in a serious relationship with him? Could he survive watching her day in and day out with another guy?

Hudson tapped his arm again and AJ glanced over. He hadn't realized they were already at the gym.

Talk to me, Hudson signed.

"Nothing to talk about," he grumbled. "Milly's goin' on a date."

What are you going to do about it?

AJ huffed. "Me? What the hell can I do about it? She's a grown woman. It's not like she's tied down or anything."

Hudson's hands were moving again. You are an idiot.

"Me? Why am I an idiot?"

Because you are willing to let her go.

"Let her go?" AJ sighed. "It's not like I'm letting her do anything. She's not mine. Never has been."

But she should be, Hudson signed.

"Maybe in my mind. But not in Milly's."

Have you told her how you feel?

AJ didn't respond. Instead, he frowned at his brother.

You love her, you dumb ass. That is obvious.

"Obvious to whom?" Certainly not Milly. And if it was, she didn't have the same feelings for him.

You have to talk to her.

Actually, he didn't have to do anything. Maybe it was time he moved on, too. Stopped acting like a love-sick jackass.

He had spent the past year wanting Milly, hoping she would realize he wasn't simply in her life because she'd gotten pregnant. Even before she'd found out, AJ had messaged her endlessly, doing his level best to find a way into her life. It was as though she had written him off completely the minute they stepped off that ship.

"Let's just go work out," AJ told Hudson. He was finished with this discussion.

If only he could be finished with Milly.

Unfortunately, things weren't that simple. Especially since Hudson was right. AJ was in love with the damn stubborn woman.

*

"HOLY SHIT, HOLY shit, holy shit," Milly squealed, staring down at her phone.

Why wasn't AJ texting her back? Why didn't he bombard her with questions? Didn't he give a shit that she was going on a date with someone else?

Well, technically, she wasn't really going on a date. It was all a ruse to get AJ to react. To see if he really did care about her the way she wanted him to.

"Relax," Dare told her. "It'll all work out."

For all intents and purposes, Dare was her brother-in-law. Being that he had married Milly's stepbrother, Noah, he was now part of her family. Didn't matter she and Noah weren't related by blood, Milly still considered him her brother.

"He didn't say anything," she argued, her eyes shooting up to him. "You told me it would work. What if he doesn't take the bait?"

What if he hated her? What if he never wanted to see her face again?

Dare chuckled. "He will. Trust me. Right about now, he's a little pissed off. Probably wondering what the fuck is going on. Give him a little time."

Milly couldn't believe she'd let Dare talk her into this. Of all the harebrained schemes, why had she thought this would work? Granted, it had seemed logical when Dare laid out the plan. Tell AJ she had a date to force him to react. At that point, they could address the situation rationally.

Instead, AJ had agreed to watch Miranda, and though he had asked what she was doing, he hadn't responded after that. Was he pissed? Hurt?

God, she hoped he wasn't hurt. That was the last thing she wanted. Milly had long ago accepted that she was in love with AJ. She didn't want to admit it, not to herself and not to anyone else, but that didn't make it less true.

"Hey," Noah greeted when he joined them in the kitchen. "I didn't know you were here. Where's Miranda?"

"She's with Cam and Gannon. They wanted to spend some time with her."

Noah glanced between her and Dare. "What are you two scheming?"

Milly had come over to her stepbrother's house to talk to Dare specifically. She hadn't realized Noah wasn't at the fire station today. Otherwise, she probably would've stuck to texting. Dare was the instigator, but Noah was the level-headed one. He would likely tell her she was out of her mind for plotting something that could so easily backfire on her.

And truth be told, Milly didn't want to hear his logical reasons right now. She was freaked out as it was.

Dare turned his head up to Noah when he approached. "No scheming. Now get over here and kiss me."

Noah chuckled but followed through with the order. He stepped up to Dare and kissed him sweetly. Milly looked away. Not because it was getting heated but more so because she couldn't stand to look at them. It seemed everyone she knew was in love and living their happy ever after while she was… She wasn't even sure what she was doing besides causing more problems.

"I'd buy that," Noah stated, "except Milly's not talking. Whenever that happens, something's wrong. Which likely means you're scheming."

Milly looked up at her stepbrother. "Your husband talked me into telling AJ I had a date."

Noah rolled his eyes and sighed. "Well, it's your fault for listening to him."

She glared at Noah. "Not helping."

He laughed. "Well, I coulda told you not to listen to him."

"Hey," Dare interjected. "Don't knock the plan just yet. Give him time."

Noah headed for the refrigerator. "He's right, though. If it's gonna work, you'll have to give him some time. Let him fester for a bit. Once he realizes what he wants, he'll be on your door step."

"Do you think it's what he wants?" Milly didn't want to sound whiny or uncertain, but when it came to AJ, that was how she felt. She wanted answers and she wanted them now.

"I do," Dare said matter-of-factly. "You can see it in the way he looks at you, Mill. He's just stubborn."

Noah chuckled. "Just like you, Mill."

"Shut up." She peered down at her phone again. "And if he's not sitting there trying to come up with a plan to win me over?" She couldn't imagine AJ would fall for this. He was likely really, really angry. Maybe even trying to figure out visitation for Miranda.

Oh, God.

"He is, I promise," Dare reassured her. "Give the guy a little time to process. First comes the anger, then the disappointment, followed by reasoning. Once he realizes he has to do something to stop you from going out, he'll confront you."

"But I'm not going out," she stated firmly. Good grief. She hadn't been on a date in … not since before she met AJ.

And she honestly hadn't had any desire to, either. Which was a first for her.

Back before Miranda was born, before she'd gotten pregnant, Milly rarely spent a weekend at home alone. She was always out. One guy or another would ask and she would accept. More often than not, she hadn't found anyone who struck her fancy, but she had at least tried.

Of course, the minute she'd met AJ, she knew he was going to be the one to bowl her over. She'd seen it in the way he looked at her, the way he touched her, kissed her.

God, she missed his kisses. Sometimes she wanted to go back in time so she could relive those few days on the cruise. Just a little more time with AJ, that was all she wanted.

"But he doesn't know that," Dare quipped. "He's probably imagining some blow-hard coming into your life and stealing you away from him. Once he's gotten past that, he'll be coming up with a plan to ensure that doesn't happen."

God. What had she done? What if this blew up in her face? What if AJ decided he would go out on a date since he thought she was?

Holy shit.

The thought of AJ out on a date… It made Milly's insides queasy. And it wasn't simply because there might be another woman in Miranda's life someday. No, this had everything to do with Milly's possessive instinct when it came to AJ. She wanted him all to herself.

"Relax," Noah said, squeezing her shoulder when he came back to the table. "Like Dare said. Give it time." He smiled. "And if it backfires, you have my permission to beat him up."

"Who?" She peered up at Noah. "AJ?"

Noah smirked, his brown eyes glittering with amusement. "No. Dare."

"Hey. That's not fair," Dare said with a wicked grin. "But it doesn't matter. It's gonna work. Just wait and see."

Unfortunately, that was all she could do.

Fourteen

GOING CAVEMAN

ENOUGH WAS ENOUGH.

AJ couldn't take it anymore.

Ever since Milly had texted to let him know she was going on a date tomorrow night, he'd been revved up. His muscles were knotted and his head ached from clenching his teeth so damn hard.

No way could he sit back and wait to see what happened when she went out with God only knew who. Probably some jackass who wouldn't know how to treat a lady if his life depended on it. Milly deserved someone who was going to take care of her. She deserved someone who would put her first.

After he got home from the gym, AJ had shaved and showered, then pulled on a pair of jeans. He had wandered around his sparse two-bedroom house wishing like hell he was with Milly and Miranda.

With a low grunt, he ran his hands through his hair.

"Fuck it." AJ headed for his bedroom, pulled on a T-shirt and his boots before grabbing his wallet, keys, and phone.

Five minutes later, he was on his way to Milly's house. He could use the excuse that he missed Miranda and wanted to spend some time with her. After all, that wasn't a lie. He did miss his daughter. Every time he was away from her, AJ could think of little else besides watching the way her little eyes lit up, her tiny hands reaching for anything and everything. She was growing up too fast.

He considered texting Milly to let her know he was on his way but decided against it. Ten minutes later, he pulled up to her house and parked his truck in the second space in the driveway.

"It's time to stop fucking around," he admonished himself as he climbed out of the truck and headed for the front door. "Time to do what you've been wanting to do for a fucking year now."

AJ rang the doorbell and waited, glancing around at the pristine neighborhood with the cute little houses with emerald-green lawns. It was a nice area and he knew Milly had moved here because Gannon had moved out this way. It was a trek for her when it came to going into the office, but she didn't seem to mind.

When he heard the deadbolt unlatch, he turned back to face the door.

Milly's face appeared, her eyes wide, as though she wasn't expecting him.

"Hey." He would play it cool. Pretend he was here for Miranda.

"Hey," she said with a hesitant smile as she stepped back so he could come in.

It took a moment for his eyes to adjust to the dim light inside. The fierce May sun was still shining brightly, already hotter than hell although summer hadn't quite made it there yet.

"What brings you by?" Milly asked when she closed the door behind him.

I came to see Miranda.

Thought I'd check in.

Missed my daughter, wanted to stop by.

All were valid reasons for coming over. However, AJ couldn't seem to spit out any of the words. He was fucking tired of making excuses, tired of pretending every breath he took didn't make him ache to be here with Milly.

Milly was still staring at him, waiting for a response.

AJ took a step closer, unable to help himself.

Milly's eyes widened as she took a step back. It wasn't fear he saw reflected in her brilliant blue gaze, though.

He took another step, then another, until Milly was crowded between his big body and the wall.

"AJ...?"

"Ah, fuck, Milly." Before he could stop himself, he was cupping her face and kissing her lips.

She inhaled a sharp gasp, her hands fisting in his shirt. He briefly imagined her pushing him away, smacking him for taking more than she was offering.

However, Milly did neither of those things, because she was offering. The next thing AJ knew, Milly was kissing him back, her arms wreathing his neck as she pulled him closer.

"I've waited too damn long," he whispered between frantic kisses. He'd hoped to be cool and calm, but the moment his lips touched hers, all thought fled, all sense of decency took a backseat to the hunger that churned in his blood.

AJ tilted her head at an angle, deepening the kiss, feasting on her mouth. Their tongues dueled, her hands sliding into his hair, cupping the back of his head as she went up on her toes to meet him.

He'd forgotten how incredible it felt to kiss Milly. They hadn't kissed since the ship, and now that his mouth was on hers, he never wanted to stop.

"Where's Miranda?" he asked when he had no choice but to pull back to breathe.

"Nap." Milly was breathless, her voice barely above a whisper.

"We need to talk," he told her, his forehead pressing against hers.

A smile tugged at her mouth. "You walk in here, kiss me like a starving man, and you want to talk?"

"No, not really," he admitted with a chuckle. "But it's that or I'm going to carry you to your bedroom and strip you naked. Your call."

A shiver racked her small frame, but Milly didn't move. "I'm liking what's behind door number two."

AJ pulled back enough to look into her eyes. "What about your date?"

She shrugged, but her eyes dropped from his face.

"Milly…? Talk to me."

When she suddenly pulled away from him, AJ wanted to kick his own ass. He'd had her right where he'd wanted her for so long and he was going to ruin it by talking? Someone should relieve him of his man card, because clearly he hadn't earned it. Not when it came to Milly.

He had to follow or be left in the entryway looking like a dumb ass.

"Talk to me, Mill."

Her voice sounded lighter when she said, "You're the one who came here to talk."

Reaching for her arm, AJ stopped her retreat. He tugged until she was facing him. "No, I came here to tell you…" His voice dried up, the words on the tip of his tongue.

Although he wanted nothing more than to tell her he loved her, that he couldn't stand the thought of her going out with another man, AJ found himself tongue-tied.

At a complete loss for words.

*

ALTHOUGH AJ WAS standing right in front of her, Milly couldn't believe he was really there.

She knew he hadn't come because of Miranda. Well, not completely. It looked as though Dare's plan had worked. By telling him she had a date, Milly was forcing AJ's hand.

The way he had kissed her as though he was starving made her believe that he wanted her every bit as much as she wanted him.

Except he wanted to talk.

The way he stared at her made her feel like an asshole. She'd deceived him and she felt like shit for doing it. This wasn't the way she wanted things to work between them.

"Tell me," she insisted. If he had something to say, she wanted to hear it.

AJ's emerald-green eyes sparkled with the remnants of lust remaining from their kiss. She knew how he felt because her body was on fire, her molecules shifting into chaos, eager for more of what he had been offering just a few minutes ago.

"You can't go on a date," AJ stated.

Milly frowned. "What do you mean I can't?"

His eyes implored her, as though he wanted her to read between the lines. She couldn't do it. She needed him to spit it out, to admit that there was something between them, something real and powerful. Something that needed to be explored.

"I mean … do you think you're ready?"

Milly fought her initial reaction but she knew he could see her disbelief. Was he really going to do this?

"Ready to date?" Milly took a step back. "Why wouldn't I be?"

AJ's gaze swung toward the hallway, where Miranda's bedroom was.

"You think that, because I have a kid, I can't date?" Irritation began to consume the remaining lust.

"That's not what I'm saying."

"Then what are you saying, AJ?"

His eyes were once again fixed on her face and she saw the residual heat. He was denying his feelings for her and it was starting to piss her off.

"I don't fucking know," he growled under his breath, his face contorting with what looked to be pain.

In a signature AJ move, he thrust his hand in his dark hair and sighed before pacing across the room.

"AJ, why are you here?"

He paced right back over, his eyes narrowed, his lips a thin line. Milly would go so far as to say he looked terrified. Whatever he had to say, he didn't think she would take it well.

She had to admire the fact that he was there, though. He was confronting her, even if it wasn't in a timely manner. The way he'd kissed her said he didn't like the idea of her going out on a date with someone else. Right? Or was it merely a knee-jerk reaction? Perhaps this was all in her head. Maybe she was the one who thought there was more between them than there was.

If that was the case, she really was an idiot for pulling this stupid stunt in the first place.

"Look, AJ," she began. "About the date. I—ugh" She was cut off completely when AJ jerked her against him.

This time, when his mouth crushed hers, there wasn't an ounce of tenderness in his body. He was rough, urgent. Needy. And her body responded in kind.

"I don't want you to go on a date," he growled between drugging kisses.

AJ's arms banded around her, holding her close. It was difficult to breathe, but Milly didn't care. Who needed air? She certainly didn't. Not when she had AJ's lips on hers, his persistent tongue sweeping through her mouth.

Milly moaned, desperate to get closer. Tears threatened. Stupid, unnecessary tears. This was everything she'd wanted and she was emotionally overwhelmed by the fact that AJ was standing here, kissing her, wanting her as much as she wanted him.

She'd been an idiot to push him away all those months ago when he had reached out to see her after the cruise. But she'd been scared. Terrified of what she felt for him and unwilling to fall all the way in love with him only to have it ripped out from under her. Because that was how it worked for her. Men didn't stick around.

AJ pulled back, staring down at her face. He must've noticed that the dam was about to break, because his forehead creased.

"What's wrong, beautiful? Did I hurt you?"

She shook her head, unable to speak. Milly feared a single word would break the tattered remains of her self-control. She didn't want to cry. She didn't want him to get the wrong idea. She was happy. Overjoyed, really.

"Talk to me, Mill. Tell me what's wrong?"

Milly shook her head again and swallowed hard before pulling him back down to her so that their mouths touched. She gave in to his kiss, to the warmth of his body. He surrounded her, eased the torment she'd been battling for months.

What started out almost gentle turned into an inferno and Milly found herself trying to climb his body. AJ obviously wasn't trying to get away, but when he gripped the backs of her thighs and lifted her up, she moaned again. He held her weight as she wrapped her legs around him, her lips bruised by the passion he was emitting.

"Bedroom," she whispered, swallowing the lump in her throat. "Please, AJ."

Only when he started walking did she release the breath she'd been holding, nuzzling his neck, inhaling his intoxicating scent.

She was finally right where she wanted to be.

Fifteen

ONE NIGHT IS NOT ENOUGH

OVERWHELMED BY EVERYTHING Milly, AJ put one foot in front of the other. She'd requested to go to the bedroom and he wasn't about to disappoint her.

After all, he'd spent the past year dreaming about getting her beneath him one more time. Her laid out naked beneath him, nothing between them at all. Only this time, he wasn't going to let her go. If she welcomed him inside her body, he would insist she welcome him in her heart, too.

A year was far too long to be pining away for a woman, yet he had done exactly that. A couple of ill-timed intimate encounters hadn't done anything to ease the lust burning through him. And it damn sure hadn't stopped him from wanting to spend every waking moment with her.

AJ braced one knee on her bed, then followed her down, loving the way her legs remained securely wrapped around his hips, as though she wasn't willing to let their bodies separate.

Her hands instantly shifted to his T-shirt, jerking it upward in an effort to get it off. AJ had no choice but to release her lips. He pushed up and helped her along, tossing his shirt onto the floor. He cupped her face and resumed feasting on her mouth. He couldn't get enough of her. Wasn't sure he ever would.

When Milly shifted, he realized she was trying to get at his jeans. Chuckling, AJ broke the kiss and stared down into her eyes. The brilliant blue depths glowed with desire and need and he wanted nothing more than to fulfill her every wish, give her all she could ever want.

"Not one night, Milly," he warned. "I can't accept that."

Some of the sparkle left her gaze and a cold chill danced down his spine.

"What if you change your mind?" she asked, her voice crackling as though she truly believed he wasn't going to stick around.

"I won't," he assured her. "But one night will never be enough." He sighed. "Hell, one lifetime won't be enough."

She wiggled, attempting to push him off her.

Without using force, AJ remained where he was, refusing to move. He had her right where he wanted her. Now it was time to talk.

Milly's eyes trailed down his neck, his shoulders, over his chest. He could see she wanted him. There was no denying the physical attraction. Not on her part or his.

"Tell me what you want, Milly," he insisted.

"You." She said it as though it was obvious.

"You've got me, baby. You've had me since the first day I met you." But then she had washed her hands of him when they had come back to the States. She had ignored his calls, his texts. Every attempt he'd made went unanswered. And still, the day she told him she was pregnant, he had taken it as the opportunity he wanted it to be. Of course AJ loved his daughter. He would've been in Miranda's life no matter what. However, he wanted Miranda's mother just as much.

In fact, he had been falling in love with her more and more every day.

"Milly…" AJ leaned down and kissed her lips. The sweet smell of her went to his head. "I want all of you, beautiful."

"How do you know?"

He smiled. "Because I know."

She stared up at him, confusion making her frown. He could see her indecision. Milly wanted what he was offering, but he sensed she didn't believe it was real. Listening to her stories, AJ knew she'd had bad luck with men in her past. She was so blasé when she spoke of her previous relationships. As though sticking around through thick and thin wasn't something men did. Not where she was concerned, anyway.

However, AJ had proven himself over the past year. He'd stuck by her during her pregnancy, then after.

This time when AJ kissed her, the gloves came off. Hers and his. The chemistry that had always tethered them together was so potent it went right to his bloodstream. He was high on her, drugged by her scent, her kiss.

Although he wanted some sort of confirmation from her, he couldn't hold back any longer. He needed to taste her, to remind himself of those days so long ago when he'd had her all to himself.

He released her lips and inched down her body, his tongue trailing over her warm skin. He felt the pulse in her neck, heard her ragged breaths as he moved lower.

When his lips trailed over the swell of her breast, he tugged the cup on her bra, freeing one luscious mound. AJ feasted on her, loving the way she writhed beneath him, her hips gyrating as she tried to get closer. He would give her everything she wanted, that much he knew.

And right now, Milly wanted the release he could offer and he wasn't about to let her down.

*

AJ WAS SAYING all the words Milly had longed to hear. She wanted everything he was willing to give, but she was terrified. Scared that he would be in her life one minute and gone the next.

That was the way it worked for her. Every man in her life except for her father had abandoned her. She'd never even been given a chance to get close to them.

"Oh…" Milly arched her back when AJ teased her nipple with his teeth. She could feel the imaginary tug between her nipple and her clit. It drove her mad, the need to feel him inside her. As much as she loved foreplay, she wanted to feel him, to hold him close while he delivered the ecstasy that had brought them together in the first place.

Not caring if she looked like a wanton hussy, Milly twitched and twisted, trying to get him where she needed him most. AJ was having none of that, though. He was patient as he worked her body, his lips and tongue bringing all those nerve endings to life.

"AJ ... I need you."

"I know, beautiful." He pushed up on his knees and placed a hand in the center of her chest to keep her down. "But this is my time right now."

Milly moaned in frustration, which only made him laugh. His eyes were heated, his smile wickedly sexy.

Her gaze roamed over every delicious inch of him. All that smooth skin covering the rippling muscle beneath. In all the time she'd known him, Milly had never tired of sneaking peeks of his ridiculously hot bod. The man made her mouth water. The way he moved, the way he walked. Hell, even the way he talked. She was so in lust with him it made her crazy.

Finally he worked free the button on her shorts before hopping off the bed. He wasted no time tugging her shorts down, then her panties. Milly went to work unhooking her bra.

"Beautiful, baby," he whispered as his molten green eyes trailed over her.

Milly knew she wasn't perfect. She never had been, but having Miranda had changed her body. Faint pink lines now marked her body and she knew they would never go away. However, she embraced those marks. They were subtle reminders that she had brought a life into this world.

AJ's gaze met hers and she could see the indecision in his eyes. She wasn't sure what he was battling, but a few seconds later, his rough "fuck it" made her feel invincible. He quickly stripped off his own clothes and moved over her once again.

Those emotional walls she'd been fighting crumbled when he hovered above her. Despite the heat building between them, there was something more. Something Milly had never felt before when it came to a man. There was that tightness in her chest. The one she'd experienced the day Miranda was born. As though her heart was swelling to twice its normal size because it was filled to overflowing with love.

"Are you on birth control?" he asked, his eyes locked with hers. "Not that I care. We can have a million babies, as far as I'm concerned, but that's not my decision to make."

"Yes. I am on birth control." Milly smiled. "Now."

"Do I need a condom?" he asked, his lips hovering by hers. "Because I'd give anything to feel you skin to skin."

"No." Milly lifted her head and brushed her lips to his. "No condom."

She felt the head of his cock press against her entrance, and she was so eager to feel him, her hips moved of their own accord, trying to bring him inside her.

AJ's lips fused to hers. A soft, heartbreakingly gentle kiss ensued as he pushed inside her. Slowly. Ever so slowly.

Her body came alive in a way only AJ could make happen. Milly wrapped her arms around him and fought the need to fuck him hard and rough. That would come next. Right now, this was what she needed. To feel him inside her. Every shift, every thrust. She wanted what he was offering.

He groaned against her lips as he sank all the way inside. Milly sucked in a breath. The feeling was intense. A small amount of pain, but only because of the glorious way he was stretching her muscles.

"God, baby," he whispered. "I've missed you so fucking much."

Milly knew what he meant. It wasn't that they'd been apart. They had seen each other almost every day since Miranda was born. But this … connected to him this way. Every minute since the last time they'd done this had felt like a lifetime.

Of course, the slow, leisurely pace couldn't last long. The lust was too potent, the need too overwhelming. AJ rolled his hips, sliding deep, retreating. He continued for what felt like days. Milly braced his hips with her knees, wanting him to give her more. It wasn't enough but it was too much at the same time. Her body sang with pure, raw pleasure.

"Milly … beautiful…" AJ lifted his head and stared down at her. "Fuck, baby."

And that was exactly what he did.

AJ impaled her roughly, slamming his hips forward.

"Yes!" Milly's eyes closed, her head tilted back.

He did it again, his thrusts sharp and eager. As though he couldn't hold back any longer.

This was what Milly missed with AJ. The man had worked her over those nights they'd spent together. He had given her everything he had, showing her a world of ecstasy she hadn't known existed.

And while she appreciated the love she could see in his gaze, she wanted the raw power this man wielded. She wanted him to unleash on her, to take her to new heights.

"More," she pleaded.

He stared down at her, his eyes so hot she thought she might combust from the intensity.

"Hands over your head," he ordered.

Milly lifted her arms, doing as he instructed.

One of his hands bracketed her wrists and held her in place as he drove into her. Once, twice...

AJ fucked her hard and deep, his pelvis slamming into hers as he rode her so beautifully.

Milly panted and moaned, a slew of unintelligible words escaping as she begged and pleaded for more. He drove her right out of her mind, filling her, stretching her, making her wild. The lust consumed her, driving out all thought until the only thing she knew was the feel of him.

What started out sweet turned brutal and perfect.

An orgasm rocketed through her, shocking her with its intensity. It overrode her mind. She screamed as glorious sensation slammed into her.

"Fuck, baby," AJ growled. "Do that again. Come all over my cock so I can come inside you."

He fucked her. Harder, faster, deeper, the bed rocking with every punishing thrust.

When he lifted, kneeling between her legs, Milly thought for a second he would stop, but he didn't. Instead, he grabbed her hips, holding her still as he drove into her over and over, claiming her in a way she'd never been claimed before.

His hair fell over his eyes, his chest heaving as his breaths raced in and out of his lungs. Gone was the sweet man who had tried to seduce her with words. In his place, the alpha male hell-bent on driving her over the edge again and again.

Milly's insides coiled again, tighter this time. She fought to draw air into her lungs as she peered up at him. The strain on his face was animalistic. As though he'd been reduced to nothing more than a man who was intent on making her see stars.

Another orgasm ignited, barreling down on her. Like the first, Milly couldn't stop it, but she was prepared, allowing the beautiful electricity to burst forth from her core until she was consumed by heat and warmth and a love so strong she wasn't sure she would survive it.

AJ fell on top of her, his hips driving forward one last time as he roared his release.

It was powerful and perfect and Milly silently prayed that this was only the beginning.

Sixteen

MARRY ME

AJ FELL TO his side and tugged Milly close. Her ass pressed against his cock and he held her tightly.

"I love you, Milly," he whispered.

Her breath hitched and her arm tightened around his but she didn't say anything.

Sighing, AJ tried to be okay with the fact that she didn't tell him she loved him, too. He wanted to hear it. Not only because he loved her but because he knew Milly loved him. He could see it in her eyes.

He pressed a kiss to her shoulder and that was when he realized she was shaking. Lifting his head, he peered over at her face. She was crying.

Aw, fucking hell. He'd made her cry.

Son of a bitch.

"Milly? What's wrong, beautiful? Talk to me."

She shook her head rapidly and wiped her eyes. "N-nothing's wrong."

When she laughed, something inside him eased.

"I'm an emotional mess, AJ."

"I think that's a little dramatic," he teased.

She laughed again and rolled over until she was facing him. He rested his head back on the pillow and stared into her beautiful eyes.

"I have to tell you something," she said quickly.

"What's that?"

Her eyes closed and she sighed. "I didn't really have a date."

He pulled back enough to see more of her face. When she opened her eyes, he smiled. "No?"

Milly shook her head. "I lied. But I had a good reason."

"And that was?"

"Because I wanted you to figure it out for yourself."

He was confused. "Figure what out?"

"That ... I wanted something more."

"Probably would've been easier to say something," he suggested, grinning.

"You're not mad?"

"No." Not even a little. "I'm glad you did."

"Why? Because you were clueless?"

He laughed. "I wouldn't go that far."

"Okay, fine. Maybe I was the clueless one."

"That's better."

Milly laughed and smacked his chest.

"I do love you, Milly," he told her. "I want to spend the rest of my life with you. Raising Miranda and all the other babies we have."

"How many?" she asked on a sob. "How many babies?"

He shrugged. "As many as you want."

They could have a dozen for all he cared. He loved Miranda more than anything and having more babies with Milly made his heart swell.

"I love you, AJ," she whispered, her hand coming up to cup his cheek. "I'm not good at showing it."

Oh, she was better than she thought, but he didn't tell her that.

For the longest time, they remained just like that, on their sides, staring back at one another.

AJ knew he should've considered all the right ways to propose to this woman. Getting dressed up, taking her to dinner, getting down on one knee. He should probably ask her father's permission first. Maybe he should wait until Miranda was there so she could witness it, even if she was too small to ever remember.

But AJ wasn't willing to wait even another minute longer.

Cupping her face, he moved closer. "Marry me, Milly. Let me spend the rest of my life making you happy. I don't want to spend another day away from you."

Her smile broke his heart. The tears that pooled in her eyes made his stomach clench.

"Yes," she whispered. "I'll marry you, AJ."

Energized by her response, AJ moved over her once more. He rested his weight on his elbows as he kissed her sweetly.

"I love you," he said between kisses. "I've loved you since the day I met you."

She pressed kisses to his jaw, his neck. "I love you, too. And I'm sorry that we wasted so much precious time."

He grinned, bringing her mouth back to his. "Well, I'll let you make up for it somehow."

Milly chuckled. "Will you now?"

"Oh, yeah."

"What do you say we start now?"

AJ aligned their bodies and pushed inside her. "Like this?"

Milly moaned, her arms wreathing his neck. "Just like this."

So, that was what he did. AJ loved her and he vowed to spend the rest of his life making a whole lot more memories with this beautiful woman.

Epilogue

HAPPILY EVER AFTER

October 31, 2018

TEAGUE BALLARD (yes, he had taken Hudson's name) headed for the front door when the bell rang, signaling another group of trick-or-treaters.

Everyone had come over to Cam and Gannon's for Halloween at Milly's insistence. Because she had offered to cook them dinner, Teague hadn't seen a reason not to show up. Plus, he liked to hang out with the gang, more so the kids, but he didn't share that with anyone. Regardless of who was there, it was always interesting with the little ones under foot.

Teague pulled the door open and glanced at the group of kids standing there expectantly. A witch, a ballerina, and a little boy in a Superman costume peered up at him. "Trick or treat."

Smiling down at them, Teague grabbed huge handfuls of candy and passed it out. After a few shy thank-yous, the kids moved back down the driveway toward the next house.

He stood there for a moment, watching them leave. He imagined those would one day be the kiddos currently in the house behind him. Walking side by side, best friends going out to pilfer candy from strangers.

What a life.

On occasion, Teague found himself reflecting on how they'd all gotten to this point. Living on the lake, working hard but playing harder, hanging out, enjoying one another's company. Every day was new and interesting and Teague no longer spent any time dwelling on his past or the pain he'd endured growing up. It was as though he'd been reborn and this was his family.

Everyone was married now. Cam and Gannon, Dare and Noah, Roan and Seg, Milly and AJ. As well as him and Hudson. Along with wedded bliss, there were babies. Roan and Seg had Liam, who had turned two last month. Miranda was now one and a half, and Brianna, AJ and Milly's second daughter, was a whopping two months old. Plus, Collin, Cam and Gannon's adopted son, was now four and the life of the party. Not that Teague had anything against the smaller ones, but he happened to be quite fond of Collin. The kid was a hoot.

"Uncle Teague!" Collin called from behind him.

Teague turned to see the little boy racing his way. Holding out his arms, he allowed the munchkin to launch himself into his arms.

"What's up, little man?"

"I wanna hand out candy."

"You wanna hand it out? Or you wanna eat it?"

Collin grinned slyly. Teague had taken Collin to several houses on the block earlier this evening for his chance to get his own candy. Surprisingly enough, after just four houses, Collin had said he was ready to go home so he could pass it out. He didn't seem to be fond of scrounging for candy on people's doorsteps.

So, he'd brought Collin back and allowed him to help with passing it out. Teague hadn't missed how the little boy had pocketed a Hershey miniature earlier. The kid was sneaky. Another thing Teague liked about him.

"Are they finished doing the dishes?" Teague asked Collin.

"Yep. You're safe."

Teague laughed. He'd purposely volunteered to hand out candy to keep from having to help in the kitchen. He had asked Collin to be his lookout so he knew when it was safe to go back in there.

"Good work," he told Collin as he set him on his feet. He pointed toward the candy bucket by the door. "Take whatever you want."

Collin's little fist curled around as much candy as he could get and Teague laughed.

"Only one. You've got your own bucket."

"Fine." Collin grabbed another Hershey miniature and then took off toward the back of the house, his Batman cape flapping behind him.

Yep. Their worlds had changed a lot in the past few years. Weddings, babies, even a Stanley Cup win for Seg. It was a whole new world. One Teague found himself never wanting to leave. Over time, these people had become his family, giving him everything he'd spent his entire life missing.

While it had taken some time and quite a few mountains they'd had to scale, everyone had come out the other side better off.

Cam, while still reckless at heart, had toned it down because Gannon now provided him the adrenaline rush he'd always craved.

Of course, Dare was still fearless, launching headfirst into everything, but Noah was there to rein him in and keep him in line. The two of them were made for each other.

As for him and Hudson ... well, Teague would just say that even if his husband could talk, Teague would still have the ability to render him speechless. He lived every day to make that man happy. In return, he went to sleep every night knowing he had the best of everything with that man.

Roan and Seg ... they were an entirely different story. Seg still claimed he was harmless, but it was obvious Roan knew better. The man had blown in like a whirlwind, knocking Roan right off his feet but catching him long before he could ever fall.

And AJ and Milly had given clueless a whole new meaning. Even Teague had seen what was transpiring between them, even when they hadn't. He was happy that they'd finally given in.

It was right out of a storybook. Or maybe five. A happily ever after for all.

God. When the hell had he started waxing poetic about love? He blamed Hudson. The man made him all wishy-washy.

Speaking of…

Hudson appeared in the hallway, moving toward him with purpose.

Teague grinned, backing up against the front door as the big man stalked closer.

What are you doing? Hudson signed.

"Nothing. What are you doing?"

Making sure you're not causing trouble.

Teague laughed. "Babe, I'm always causing trouble. That's why you love me."

Hudson pressed him up against the door, a wicked gleam making his emerald eyes sparkle.

Teague knew that look.

It meant he was getting lucky tonight.

Well, luckier. Because he was already pretty damn lucky.

They all were.

***

Want to see some fun stuff related to my books, you can find extras on my website. Or how about what's coming next? Find more at: www.NicoleEdwardsAuthor.com

If you're interested in keeping up to date on any new releases and preorders, you can sign up for my notification newsletter on my website under "Subscribe". This only goes out when I've got a book coming up.

Want a simple, fast way to get updates on new releases? You can also sign up for text messaging. If you are in the U.S. simply text NICOLE to 64600 or sign up on my website. I promise not to spam your phone. This is just my way of letting you know what's happening because I know you're busy, but if you're anything like me, you always have your phone on you.

And last but certainly not least, if you want to see what's going on with me each week, sign up for my weekly Hot Sheet! It's a short, entertaining weekly update of things going on in my life and that of the team that supports me. We're a little crazy at times and this is a firsthand account of our antics.

You can also find me here:

Twitter: @NicoleEAuthor

Facebook: /Author.Nicole.Edwards

Instagram: NicoleEdwardsAuthor

Acknowledgments

First and always, I have to thank my wonderfully patient husband who puts up with me every single day. If it wasn't for him and his belief that I could (and can) do this, I wouldn't be writing this today. He has been my backbone, my rock, the very reason I continue to believe in myself. I love you for that, babe.

A big thank you to my betas, my proofreaders, and my street team! You ladies make sure it's all top-notch and in people's hands. I appreciate everything you do for me.

I can't forget my copyeditor, Amy at Blue Otter Editing. Thank goodness I've got you to catch all my punctuation, grammar, and tense errors.

Nicole Nation 2.0 for the constant support and love. You've been there for me from almost the beginning. This group of ladies has kept me going for so long, I'm not sure I'd know what to do without them.

And, of course, YOU, the reader. Your emails, messages, posts, comments, tweets... they mean more to me than you can imagine. I thrive on hearing from you, knowing that my characters and my stories have touched you in some way keeps me going. I've been known to shed a tear or two when reading an email because you simply bring so much joy to my life with your support. I thank you for that.

About Nicole Edwards

New York Times and *USA Today* bestselling author Nicole Edwards is a hybrid author who has published over 50 books since 2012. Nicole lives in Pflugerville, Texas with her husband and their youngest of three children. Her oldest two have left the nest, but Nicole does her best to keep them close by. Nicole also keeps busy with four rambunctious dogs of her own. When she's not writing about sexy alpha males, she can often be found with a book in hand, spending time with her kids and her granddaughter, or making an attempt to keep the dogs happy. You can find her hanging out on Facebook and interacting with her readers - even when she's supposed to be writing.

By Nicole Edwards

Alluring Indulgence Series

Kaleb
Zane
Travis
Holidays with the Walker Brothers
Ethan
Braydon
Sawyer
Brendon

The Walkers of Coyote Ridge Series

Curtis
Jared
Hard to Hold
Hard to Handle
Beau

Austin Arrows Series

Rush
Kaufman

Club Destiny Series

Conviction
Temptation
Addicted
Seduction
Infatuation
Captivated
Devotion
Perception
Entrusted
Adored
Distraction

Dead Heat Ranch Series

Boots Optional
Betting on Grace
Overnight Love
Jared

Devil's Bend Series

Chasing Dreams
Vanishing Dreams

Office Intrigue Series

Office Intrigue
Intrigued Out of the Office
Their Rebellious Submissive
Their Famous Dominant
Their Ruthless Sadist

Pier 70 Series

Reckless
Fearless
Speechless
Harmless
Clueless

Sniper 1 Security Series

Wait for Morning
Never Say Never
Tomorrow's Too Late

Southern Boy Mafia/Devil's Bend Series

Beautifully Brutal
Without Regret
Beautifully Loyal
Without Restraint

Standalone Novels

Unhinged Trilogy
A Million Tiny Pieces
Inked on Paper
Bad Reputation
Bad Business

Naughty Holiday Editions

2015
2016